THE R DELIVERANCE

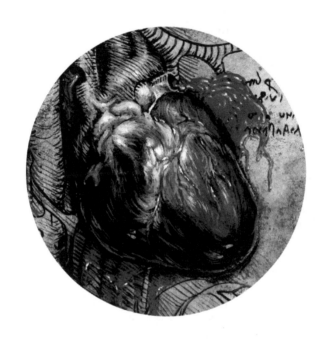

Brian Keene

deadite
press

DEADITE PRESS
P.O. BOX 10065
PORTLAND, OR 97296
www.DEADITEPRESS.com

AN ERASERHEAD PRESS COMPANY
www.ERASERHEADPRESS.com

ISBN: 978-1-62105-177-0

Acknowledgements

For this edition of The Rising: Deliverance, my thanks to Jeff Burk, Rose O'Keefe, and everyone else at Deadite Press; Paul Goblirsch; Russell Dickerson; my pre-readers Tod Clark and Mark 'Dezm' Sylva; Cassandra Burnham; and my sons.

DEADITE PRESS BOOKS BY BRIAN KEENE

Urban Gothic
Jack's Magic Beans
Take the Long Way Home
Darkness on the Edge of Town
Tequila's Sunrise
Dead Sea
Entombed
Kill Whitey
Castaways
Ghoul
The Cage
Dark Hollow
Ghost Walk
A Gathering of Crows
Last of the Albatwitches
An Occurrence in Crazy Bear Valley
Earthworm Gods
Earthworm Gods II: Deluge
Earthworm Gods: Selected Scenes from the End of the World
The Rising
City of the Dead
The Rising: Selected Scenes from the End of the World
Clickers II (with J. F. Gonzalez)
Clickers III (with J. F. Gonzalez)
Clickers vs. Zombies (with J. F. Gonzalez)
Sixty-Five Stirrup Iron Road (with Edward Lee, Jack Ketchum, Bryan Smith, J.F. Gonzalez, Wrath James White, Ryan Harding, Nate Southard, and Shane McKenzie)

This book is dedicated to Nate Southard.

More than three hundred is always good,
but even less than that counts.

"Thou art my hiding place; thou will preserve me from trouble; thou will compass me about with songs of deliverance."
—David, *The Book of Psalms*

"Nevertheless, not what I will, but what You will."
—Jesus Christ, *The Book of Mark*

"Well, because that's what God had planned for us. That's what God wanted me to do."
—Reverend Martin, *City of the Dead*

ONE

After they began to lose track of the days, and it became obvious that whatever it was that had happened to the world wasn't going to be over anytime soon, the Reverend Thomas Martin began to pray for deliverance.

At first, the news reports had been random and sporadic—filler in between the regular stories of joblessness and stock market decline and crime and politics and war. It started with a riot at a rock and roll concert in Escanaba, Michigan. Then there was a mass murder in Ghost Island, Minnesota. That led to pandemonium in the streets of Belleville, Illinois and New York City. Then everything erupted.

When the chaos reached the tiny town of White Sulphur Springs, West Virginia, Martin, Becky and John had taken shelter inside their church. It was there that they watched things fall apart. Despite the situation outside, the power remained on and the networks kept broadcasting. Soon enough, the news had confirmed the rumors spreading across the internet—the dead were coming back to life, not as slow, shambling, mindless creatures, but rather as beings possessed. Indeed, from what Martin had witnessed with his own eyes, it was as if the corpses of the recently deceased were now inhabited by a race of supernatural deities. Demons, as they were called in his trade.

He had no reason to doubt it.

Just as he believed in God the Father, maker of Heaven and Earth, and in Jesus Christ, His only son, our Lord, so did Martin believe in the other side of the coin—Satan and his minions. Demons from the pit. The hordes of Hell. The Yin to the Yang. God had His angels and Satan had his demons.

The Bible that Martin had known and loved and taught for years was very specific on this. God ruled in Heaven, but Satan had dominion over the Earth. This had never bothered Martin before, because he knew that eventually, good always triumphed. God might sometimes work in mysterious ways, but it always balanced out in the end.

At sixty years of age, Martin had seen evil at work in the world time and time again, and he'd had his faith tested more than once. He'd walked through figurative hellfire on more than one occasion. He'd been bitten by a copperhead snake when he was seven years old, while picking raspberries for his mother to make into a pie. He'd contracted pneumonia when he was ten, and had been laid up for over a month, missing school and a winter that was fine for sledding and making snowmen. In the case of both the snakebite and the pneumonia, he'd almost died, but the good Lord had seen him through.

But that wasn't all. He'd served as a Navy chaplain during Viet Nam, and seen the horrors of war first-hand. He'd smelled burning flesh, and heard men screaming like children, and witnessed the atrocities they committed on one another—killing indiscriminately, taking ears and noses and genitalia as grisly trophies, losing their minds and their souls in a haze of drugs and alcohol and murder. He'd seen the Devil at work in the jungles. He'd seen Satan's face appear in the napalm smoke and heard his laughter in the thunder of the mortar rounds, and knew that the Devil was alive and well on planet Earth.

And yet, despite everything he'd witnessed, Martin had made it back home alive by the grace of God—safe, sound and sane. Soon after his return to the United States, he'd gone to work for and alongside the Reverend Martin Luther King, attracted not just by the man's civil rights work, but by his efforts to end both poverty and the Vietnam War. Martin had felt a strange sense of prideful glee that his last name was the same as the Reverend King's first name. He'd remembered being younger, and listening to the speech on the steps of the Lincoln Memorial. Martin had shared in the dream, and was now working for that dream. And then, on a gloomy April day almost a year after his return from Vietnam, he'd seen that dream gunned down in Memphis, Tennessee. Perhaps it had been James Earl Ray who pulled the trigger that sent the bullet smashing into King's jaw and shattering his spine, but it had been the Devil that guided the assassin's hand.

But there had been divine providence in even that act of evil, for after the assassination, Martin had returned here to White Sulphur Springs, West Virginia, and had become pastor of the very church he was now hiding out in. He'd married his wife, Chesya, and they'd had two fine sons, Mark and William. Mark had died in Desert Storm. William had moved to Los Angeles and gotten in trouble with the law and was now doing hard time for manslaughter. And Chesya had passed five years ago after a battle with breast cancer.

His faith had gotten him through all of this and more. But now, for the first time, Martin wondered if that faith would be enough. He needed it, clung to it as a drowning man would cling to a lifejacket. Yes, he'd been through a lot in his life, and had always emerged stronger, both in body, mind and spirit, but none of the tests the Lord had given him over the years were as fundamental or encompassing as the one he faced now.

The last thing he'd seen before the news stopped broadcasting was a press briefing with the Secretary of State, who was filling in for the President. It became apparent to all just why the Secretary of State was fulfilling this role when, live on camera, the reanimated President darted toward the podium, spewing obscenities, and proceeded to slaughter the Secretary of State live on camera. The camera actually zoomed in as the Zombie-in-Chief clamped down on the victim's arm, biting through his suit sleeve and into the flesh beneath. One Secret Service agent drew his weapon on the former President. A second agent then shot the first. Chaos descended as more agents exchanged gun-fire and reporters scrambled. The Vice-President, it was re-ported, suffered a fatal heart attack following the press conference. Following that came a news report that both the House and the Senate had been overrun by zombies. Then the stations went off the air and the power died.

If those final reports didn't prove that the Devil's minions were working overtime, all Martin had to do was look outside the walls of his own church. It was, quite literally, Hell on Earth. And here he was, living in the midst of it. So yes, while he'd had his faith tested before, it had never been like this. Still, as Martin was fond of telling his congregation, the good Lord didn't waste his time testing those who didn't have much to offer. He just wondered what else he could offer at his age in a world gone in-sane. His parishioners were scattered—either dead or in hiding. Other than John and Becky, he had no one to minister to. What did God need him to do now?

Speak to me, Lord, he prayed. *Show me what you need of me. Reveal your will and let me know your mind. And if you don't need me, then please deliver me from this place. Deliver us from evil, Lord. Deliver—*

"A penny for your thoughts, Reverend?"

Martin jumped, so startled that he rapped his elbow against the wooden railing he'd been kneeling in front of. He winced as his forearm went numb.

"I'm sorry," Becky Gingerich, who'd been the church organist for the last seven years and a parishioner long before that, apologized. "I didn't mean to scare you. I thought you heard me come in."

"No," Martin said. "I was busy praying. But it's okay, Rebecca. Although, to be honest, I don't know that my thoughts are worth a penny."

"Oh, I bet they are. At least to me."

Smiling, Martin slowly got to his feet. The arthritis in his knees and ankles flared up as he did, competing with the numbness in his arm.

"I made dinner," Becky said. "Chicken soup and some crackers. John's already eating. We figured you might want to join us."

"That sounds like a plan." Martin's stomach growled. He hadn't realized he was hungry until then. Not for the first time, he found himself surprised at Becky's ability to guess his needs, even before he himself was aware of them.

Becky smiled, and Martin felt himself blushing. Then the organist blushed, as well. Clearing his throat, Martin turned his glance to the cross hanging above the altar. A life-sized wooden Jesus stared down at them.

Martin nodded at the figure. "We'll finish this later, Lord."

If God heard him, He didn't respond. Of course, Martin reflected, the Lord wasn't much for direct response these days anyway. Gone were the burning bushes and the giant, disembodied hands that came down from the sky and wrote on walls. These days, God didn't send armies of angels. All he sent was courage and peace and strength.

"I wish it was more," Becky said, once again interrupting Martin's thoughtful reverie. "You and John must both be getting tired of canned soup all the time."

"We make do with what we have," Martin replied, his tone gentle. "The three of us were lucky enough to take shelter here in the church, and the Sunday School pantry was well-stocked. The Lord has provided. It could be a lot worse. Think of how it must be for some of the other folks holed up out there. I'd be willing to bet not all of them are lucky enough to have food and water wherever it is they're hiding."

13

"That's true. Do you… do you think there *are* more out there? Hiding? Alive?"

"We must have faith that there are."

She frowned, her forehead creasing and the tiny wrinkles around her blue eyes becoming more pronounced. Although she didn't say it, Martin knew that Becky was thinking about her loved ones. She had a daughter who attended West Virginia State University in Morgantown, and a son who was in the Army. Becky hadn't heard from either of them since the Rising had started. She had, however, received a series of desperate, plaintive text messages from her ex-husband, who, after ten years apart from her and a second marriage, had apparently decided that the end of the world was a good time to tell his ex-wife that he'd never stopped loving her and begging her to forgive him for all the things he'd done while they were married. A tearful Becky had texted him back and told him that he was forgiven, but she'd never received a response in return. Martin supposed that the silence was probably more heart-wrenching than the original message had been. She'd tried to play her concerns off to Martin and John, proposing that her ex had probably gotten drunk and passed out, but the unspoken assumption was that something bad had happened to him, preventing him from responding.

"And besides," Martin said, trying to cheer her up, "you do more with a can of soup and some dry old crackers than most gourmet chefs could do with an entire pantry of organic foods at their fingertips. You've got talent, Rebecca. And I'm not just talking about your skills with the piano."

Beaming, she glanced at the organ, which had sat silent since the siege began. They'd been reluctant to make any sound that might alert the things outside to their presence inside the church.

"I've got to do something," she said. "Keeping busy seems to help. And I like cooking for you both."

"We like it, too. Now come on, before John eats it all."

As they walked down the center aisle, the pain in his arm subsided. Martin wished the same could be said of the aches in his joints. Their footfalls echoed in the empty church. Three of the pews had blankets and pillows strewn across them, where the three had made their makeshift beds. The hard wooden benches hurt Martin's back, but he'd padded them as best he could with foam play-mats from the church's nursery. The aisles between the rows of pews were half-hidden in shadow. John had used thick plywood sheeting to board over the beautiful stained glass windows, and the only source of illumination was the few meager rays of sun that peeked through the spy holes he'd drilled in each section of wood. At night, they used candles that they had found in a storage room—left over from communion and the previous year's Christmas Eve candlelight service.

Martin and Becky passed through a door into the vestibule and then walked down a flight of stairs to the church basement. Martin ran his palm along the handrail as they went down the stairs, stirring up dust. He sneezed.

"God bless you," Becky said.

"Thank you, Rebecca. He does."

"You know what one of the things I always liked about you was, Pastor?"

"Hmm?"

"Sometimes you call me Rebecca. My mother used to call me that, but everybody else in this town just called me Becky."

"Even your husband?"

Her frown returned. "He called me other things, most of which I'd rather not repeat."

They made their way through the Sunday School rooms and into the kitchen where John, the church's janitor, groundskeeper and all-around handyman, was seated at a

15

card table, loudly slurping chicken soup from a paper cup. His dentures sat on the table beside him. Becky clicked her tongue.

"John Amos Kuhn, you get those nasty old things off that table right now! Other people have to eat here too, you know."

His shoulders slumped at her reproach. "They're not nasty. They're clean. I brush them every night before bed. Although I reckon I won't be wearing them much longer. I'm just about out of denture cream."

The soup bubbled inside its saucepan, which was sitting atop a kerosene heater. With no electricity to run the microwave or the oven, Becky had resorted to using the heater to cook their meals. John had assured them that they had enough kerosene stored in the church's boiler room to last them through winter, though he held the opinion that they wouldn't be trapped inside the building that long. The heater had been turned off after the meal was prepared, but the warmth still radiated from it, wafting against Martin's legs as he brushed by it.

"Given the situation," Martin said, spooning some soup into a paper cup, "I don't know that denture cream is very high on our list of priorities, John. You might just have to go without."

"I don't know, Reverend. I've been thinking about that."

Martin and Rebecca took seats around the card table, and John paused long enough for Martin to say a brief prayer.

"Thank you for providing us with this food, Lord, and for continuing to keep us safe. In your name, we pray. Amen."

"Short and sweet," John said. "That's why I like you, Pastor Martin. You don't mess around."

Martin grinned. "Good food, good meat, good God, let's eat."

John cackled with laughter, spraying cracker crumbs from his mouth. Becky smiled, sipping her soup.

"So what were you saying, John?" Martin asked.

"You probably ain't gonna like it." The janitor sat his cup down. "I was fixing to go outside tomorrow. Make a supply run. Not just for denture cream, either. There's all kinds of stuff that we need."

Martin balked at the suggestion. "We've talked about this before, John. I don't think going outside right now would be very wise. We've all seen what these...zombies... are capable of doing."

"I wouldn't have to go far," John said. "Reckon I could make it to my place and get my pickup truck. It's only a quarter of a mile or so over yonder. Then I could swing by the convenience store out near the highway, grab what we need, and come right back here. The whole thing shouldn't take more than a half hour."

"And a lot of bad things could happen to you in that half hour. Even if you did manage to survive, you'd run the risk of leading all the zombies back here. So far, we've escaped their notice. If that changes, we'll have a tough time surviving. We're not equipped to fight them off if they get inside the church. We've got the shotgun and not much else."

"I think it's worth the risk, Pastor. Long as I creep along and stay behind cover, I should be able to make it to my house okay. And then, when I get the truck, I can just outrun any of them."

"I don't know, John. What do we need that's so important? The pantry is pretty well stocked."

"Yeah, but we could use more bottled water. I don't know about you two, but I'm tired of taking sponge baths. And I reckon Becky would like to use more than a quarter of a bottle when she washes the pots and pans. I'd like to have enough water on hand that we could fill up a barrel or something and take a bath."

Martin shrugged. "Do we have a barrel?"

"I could put something together," John said. "Reckon if

17

I poke around in the boiler room, I can find an old washtub leftover from one of the youth group's car washes or something."

"Couldn't you fill it with rainwater, instead? Maybe we could put it up on the roof of the church?"

"No offense, Reverend, but with all the toxic crap floating around in the air, I'd rather stink than bathe in rainwater. For all we know, that might be what's causing this epidemic."

"I don't think so," Martin replied. "I think it's something else."

John shrugged. "Maybe it is. But we ain't gonna find out sitting in here."

"What else do we need?" Becky asked. "What else would you get if you went on a supply run?"

"More food wouldn't hurt. I mean, I know we've got plenty now, but it never hurts to plan ahead, right? And we could use some more hardware—lumber and stuff like that. And weapons. As you said, Pastor, we've only got the shotgun. I could get my hunting rifles from the house. And other stuff, too. Batteries, first aid supplies, matches, more blankets, duct tape—"

Martin interrupted the litany. "Duct tape? Why would we need duct tape, John?"

"Well, come on, Reverend. It's the end of the world. You've got to have duct tape!"

Their laughter eased the slowly-building tension, and also revealed a lot about them to each other. Martin chuckled, grinning. Becky quietly smiled and covered her mouth with her hand. John slapped his knee and brayed laughter. They returned to their meal. Then, after a few moments, Martin spoke again.

"I just don't think it's a good idea, John. My mind hasn't changed on that. I think we should just stay put until help comes or until the situation resolves itself. I was thinking earlier about the Reverend Martin Luther King's 'I've Been to the Mountaintop' speech. Do you know it?"

John nodded. "Sure. Everybody does, except maybe the kids today."

"He gave that speech just before he died. He said he didn't know what would happen next. He predicted there were difficult days ahead, but that it didn't matter to him. He wanted to live a long life, but he wasn't concerned about that because, in the end, he was more dedicated to serving God's will. So am I. So should the two of you be. We're safe here, by the grace of God. This is where he wants us. I don't see any point in testing that right now. I vote we stay inside."

Martin hadn't meant it as an edict, but his tone was firm. Neither Becky nor John challenged him. Becky simply returned to her soup. John stared at the tabletop for a moment and then shrugged. They ate in silence.

***

That night, they lay there in the church, resting on the hard, wooden pews. Instead of sleeping, they listened to the moans and curses and taunts of the dead outside. Glass broke, but the plywood held. The doorknob was tried, and then something slammed against the door. All three of them remained quiet. Martin clutched the shotgun and prayed.

Deliver us from evil, Lord. Deliver us from this nightmare. Help me prove to John and Rebecca that I was right about Your will. Don't let us become dinner for those things outside.

Martin heard John shifting around in the darkness, as if he was uncomfortable. When Martin peered over the top of the pew, he noticed that the janitor was clenching his privates with one hand.

"I've got to pee," John whispered.

After almost an hour, the creatures moved on, apparently convinced that the church was deserted. John stood up and quietly hurried downstairs to the bathroom. Martin and Becky waited.

"Do you think they're really gone?" she asked, leaving her own bedroll and sitting down next to him in his pew.

"They seem to be," Martin whispered. "I don't hear anything."

"Maybe they're just trying to trick us."

"I suppose it's possible."

"That's how they got Hannah Turnbill. One of them pretended to be her daughter. Well, I guess it was her daughter. Or used to be, at least. I saw it while I was on my way here. Her daughter was knocking on the door, and calling out for her mother. Hannah opened the door to let her in, and…"

Becky's voice faded. She tried to speak, but all that came out was a choked sob. Without thinking about it, Martin put an arm around her shoulder and squeezed. Becky leaned in close against him. He was struck by how wonderful her hair smelled. Then his thoughts turned to Chesya, and he felt a pang of guilt. Even though she'd been gone a long time, he still loved her, and he didn't like the thought of her staring down from Heaven and wondering just what in the heck he thought he was doing, making time with the church organist. Sitting there with Becky felt too much like cheating, even if it was only her memory that he was being unfaithful to. With a small sigh, he slowly disengaged himself and stood up.

"Let's check," he said. "We just have to make sure we're quiet."

They tiptoed over to one of the windows and approached it with caution. Martin paused, listening. He heard no sounds from outside. Slowly, he put his eye to the peephole and peered out into the darkness. The street around the church was empty, as were the church grounds. So were the backyards of the homes surrounding the church, as well as the nearby baseball diamond. Beyond that was a cornfield.

The stalks swayed in the breeze. The mountains dominated the horizon, dark and foreboding. Martin had often thought to himself that there was nowhere in West Virginia where you couldn't see mountains. They'd always brought him comfort until now. These days, especially at night, the mountains reminded him of prison walls. That made him think of William. He wondered if his son was still alive, or if he'd gone to join his brother and mother on the other side. Both prison and Heaven seemed like viable alternatives to becoming one of the walking dead. But what if William was still locked up? What if he was starving to death inside his cell? The thought made Martin shudder.

He tried to think of happier things. He remembered the first time he and Chesya had taken the boys to the beach. That made him smile, but the expression was sad. He longed to see the ocean again. He'd always enjoyed vacations at the shore, but of course, there would be no more vacations in the near future.

The moon was almost full and cast a pale light over the surroundings, making everything seem stark and surreal. A headless corpse lay half-out of a nearby culvert. Martin was sure it hadn't been there earlier in the day. The head lay nearby. He couldn't be sure, but he thought he saw the eyes still moving.

Other than the moonlight, there was very little illumination. A few scattered streetlights were still working, but Martin couldn't figure out why. If the power was off, shouldn't they be out, too. And if they operated on a different circuit, then why weren't all of them on? In the distance, far beyond the cornfield, he saw the soft yellow glow of the sodium lights that overlooked the car dealership and strip mall that sat next to the highway exit. He wondered if perhaps the power was on at the dealership. If so, were they better off moving there?

He closed his eyes and searched his feelings, hoping for

some guidance from the Lord. After a moment, he opened them again, and found that the disembodied head was indeed staring at him. Worse, the mouth was pulled back in a sneer. Martin quickly turned away, looking toward the car dealership again. A shiver ran through him. Becky must have noticed it.

"Are you okay, Reverend?"

She reached out and stroked his arm with her fingernails. The sensation was at once soothing and exciting. Martin shivered again, but this time, it had nothing to do with discomfort or fear. Before he could respond, John returned from the restroom. They both turned to look at him, and Becky dropped her arm to the side.

"Anything out there?" John whispered.

Martin shook his head. "Nothing. The streets are quiet… for now, at least."

John joined them at the window and peered outside. "Might be a good time to try making a break for it. I was thinking about it some more after dinner. How do we know this is going on everywhere? I mean, we saw some stuff on the news, but it wouldn't be the first time the mainstream media lied about things."

Martin took a deep breath. "John, we've seen those things in action for ourselves. It isn't some Hollywood movie. They're real."

"I ain't saying they aren't. But maybe this is just a localized problem. Maybe the government has us cordoned off. I think we should get my truck and try to make it to Beckley or Lewisburg, or maybe even Richmond. There's bound to be help there."

"You saw what happened at the White House," Becky said. "That's a lot farther away than Richmond."

"Yeah, but I don't reckon that means it's like this everywhere, Becky. All we got to do is make it to a safe zone."

"But we don't know where that is," Becky objected. "You're just guessing, John. What if there is no safe zone? For all we know, it's like this everywhere!"

Martin realized that their voices were growing louder. He held up his hands to quiet them both.

"One thing is for sure," he said. "We're not going to solve this tonight. John, I agree with you that it looks relatively safe outside. But that's only as far as we can see. Those things are still lurking around somewhere out there, and you're too tired to outrun them if they find you. I suggest we talk about this more tomorrow. Fair enough?"

John nodded slowly, and when he responded, his tone was sullen.

"I reckon so, Pastor. Won't hurt none to sleep on it."

"There you go. Good man."

The three of them returned to their pews and made themselves as comfortable as possible. They lit no candles or lamps. Becky was the first to fall asleep. Martin heard her breathing in the darkness, whistling softly each time she inhaled through her nose. John was next, succumbing to slumber only a few minutes after Becky. His was a restless sleep, full of tossing and turning and half-muttered snatches of words. Each time he moved, the pew creaked beneath him. Eventually, he lay still and snored.

Martin lay on his back, put his hands behind his head, and stared at the ceiling. Then he thought about Chesya. And Rebecca. A part of him he'd long that dead now stirred, but the sensation was useless. Briefly, he considered waking Becky up, and seeing if she'd be interested, but then he talked himself out of it. Finally, he closed his eyes and prayed some more.

Deliver us, Lord. Make your will known to me. Help me to understand why you've brought us to safety here, and what you expect of us next. I am John and Rebecca's guardian, and I do not shirk from the task. I never have. But what good can a shepherd do watching over his flock if he doesn't know what comes next? Help me, Father. Tell me what you want me to do. Deliver me from this evil that is all around us.

It occurred to Martin that something was missing from the night—the ever-present sound of insects. West Virginia was full of nature's night songs, and one always heard them, unless you were in a city like Charleston or Morgantown. In the Spring, the night echoed with spring peepers. In the summer and fall, it rang with crickets, locusts and other bugs. But not anymore. He tried to remember how long it had been since he'd heard them, and couldn't decide. The absence made the night stranger and more sinister.

His crumpled khakis and black shoes were both dirty. His preacher's collar felt rough beneath his yellow sweater. Not for the first time, Martin wished for a change of clothes.

Eventually, his hands began to hurt. His arthritis was getting worse, and Martin's painkillers were at home on the other side of town. As far as he was concerned, they might as well have been on the bottom of the ocean. He shifted, trying to get comfortable, but it was no use. Each movement brought fresh aches and pains. He stared at the ceiling some more, listened to his companions breathe, and thought about what life had been like before this. Then he closed his eyes and prayed again. The only thing he did not do was sleep.

As he'd done every night since they'd taken shelter inside the church, Martin used his Scofield Reference Bible for a pillow. It wasn't the most comfortable pillow in the world, but it was a comfort.

It kept him from crying until the morning, and for Martin, that was enough.

TWO

Martin had to admit, with John's help, they'd done a pretty good job of securing the church. Indeed, it wasn't really a church anymore as much as it was an impregnable fortress.

A church doesn't have to be a building, he reminded himself. *It's simply a place where people congregate to worship the Lord. A church is where God is. Nothing more. Nothing less. A church can be a living room or a backyard or an alley. If God is there, then it's a church.*

He wondered if God was still with them now. Martin wanted to believe it to be so, but for the first time in his Christian life, he was beginning to have doubts. Not that Martin could blame Him. After all, if he was God, he wouldn't want to hang around White Sulphur Springs anymore, either.

Because things were definitely getting worse around here.

They'd awoken that next morning to the sound of a motorcycle engine. Competing with that noise was the baying of what sounded like a pack of wild dogs, or perhaps coyotes. All three of them jumped up from their beds and ran to the peepholes, only to confirm that there were indeed both dogs and coyotes in the pack—except that it wasn't a live pack at all. It was a pack of zombies.

About a dozen undead curs chased a long-haired man on a motorcycle. The bike had Virginia tags, and none of them recognized the driver. He wore no helmet, so all three of them got a good look at his features as he sped past the church. He was young, maybe in his mid-twenties, and absolutely terrified. As well he should be, not only because

25

of his pursuers, but because the motorcycle seemed on its last leg. As he rounded the corner, the bike sputtered and choked, emitting a cloud of thick, black smoke. The rider seemed to lose control for a second, wobbling back and forth. The tires squealed on the pavement.

"Almost stalled it," John said. "He's gonna spill."

"Come on," Martin urged the driver. "Pull out! Help him, Lord."

Whether through skill or divine provenance, the biker righted himself and raced ahead again. The pack ran along behind him, barking and snarling, close enough now that Martin, Becky and John could smell them, even through the walls and fortifications. All of the animals were in various stages of decomposition. Some were missing an eye or an ear. One was missing its entire lower jaw. A few had fly-infested holes where their tails had been. Some had ugly, oozing wounds in their sides or bellies. One dog dragged its intestines along behind it like a leash, and a coyote loped along on only three legs. A Golden Labrador passed by, its skull split down the middle and its brains exposed to the open air, and yet it still functioned. A blind poodle with no eyes trailed the others, following by sound. Bringing up the rear was a lone, undead housecat, its body swollen with gases. It waddled, rather than ran, in an almost comedic pantomime of life.

"My God," John gasped. "If that don't beat all. I've never seen nothing like it."

None of them had, Martin thought, but was too speechless to point it out. A pack of zombie dogs was unlike anything they'd ever experienced. He gaped at the pursuit as the motorcyclist sped off down the street. The zombies raced after him, baying and yipping. It was an odd sound, almost like...

"It can't be," Martin whispered.

He clenched his teeth and glanced at Becky and John,

only to find them staring at him. They looked as shocked as he felt.

John pointed at the window. "Was that…?"

Martin nodded. "Speech. At least, that's what it sounded like."

"I heard it, too," Becky said. "It reminded me of dogs trying to talk. Like they were trying to speak English, but lacked the vocal ability."

"Not English," Martin said. "At least, I don't think so. It reminded me of Aramaic—the language of Jesus. Or maybe something older. Maybe Sumerian? I'm not sure."

John frowned. "Sounded like dogs to me. I mean, y'all are right. It wasn't normal dog sounds. They could have been trying to talk. But Ara…? What'd you call it, Pastor?"

"Aramaic. I had to study it in seminary. I don't remember any of it now. It's a hard language to learn and even harder to remember if you don't keep practicing it. But some of the sounds those zombies were making reminded me of it."

"What does it mean, Reverend?" Becky sounded like she was about to cry. "How can that be?"

"I don't know," Martin told her. "I just don't know. In the movies, the zombies are just us—dead corpses, walking around slow and shambling and mindless. But these things… I was thinking yesterday, it's almost like they're possessed by demons. In fact, I think that may be the case."

The sound of the motorcycle engine faded. Moments later, so did the braying pack. Silence returned to the church. Martin heard a bird chirping outside and wondered if it was alive or dead.

He thought of all this now as he glanced around the church now, studying their fortifications. It was mid-afternoon, and they hadn't seen a zombie outside since the pack disappeared. Becky was downstairs reading an old copy of *The Upper Room* and John was…

It occurred to Martin that he didn't know where John

was, exactly. The janitor had been missing since shortly after break-fast, which they'd had about an hour after their encounter with the zombie dog pack. To conserve food, they limited themselves to two strict meals per day—a meager breakfast and a decent dinner, which usually consisted of various canned soups or vegetables, and either water or communion juice (the church didn't use wine).

Still wondering where John had gotten to, Martin let his eyes roam around the church. In addition to the heavy plywood covering the stained-glass windows, John had helped him take other steps to secure the building. The narthex door was bolted shut from the inside, and he and Martin had stacked three pews in front of it to help hold the door in case the zombies tried to break through. They'd done the same with the two doors downstairs, barricading both of them with strong lumber and adding additional deadbolts on the inside. The windows in the Sunday School rooms had been boarded over, as well. John had even secured the ventilation shaft over the oven in the church kitchen, and the sewer grating in the floor of the boiler room. Nothing was getting inside.

And they weren't getting out.

Martin had been adamant about this when John raised the subject again during breakfast. The janitor's insistence on leaving had increased overnight. Martin had expected the exact opposite, especially after what they'd witnessed upon waking that morning. But it had been the contrary. John was convinced that the danger was past for the moment. He'd reasoned that any zombies in the immediate vicinity had probably all joined the pursuit of the man on the motorcycle. Eventually, by the time they'd finished their single rationed cup of instant coffee, which they'd warmed atop the kerosene heater, Martin had convinced him once again to stay. Then John had sulked off, muttering under his breath.

Obviously, the strain was getting to him. How could it

not? All three of them were under an incredible amount of stress. They were hiding out inside of their church, inside of a building that had once been a place of comfort and sanctuary, while their friends, neighbors and fellow parishioners roamed around outside, looking to eat them. They had to ration their food and sleep on pews and take sponge baths. It was enough to make anyone cranky—or, if it went on long enough, to drive them insane. Martin wondered if that was what could be happening with John. This bizarre and foolhardy obsession with escaping the church and finding a safe area—could it be some form of cabin fever or psychosis, brought on by their self-imposed imprisonment?

Please, Lord. Get us out of here. How long must this go on? How long can this situation continue? Deliver us from this place, and show us Your will. In Jesus name I pray. Amen.

Martin prowled the church aimlessly. He walked past the altar rail and stood behind the podium, gazing out at the empty pews. He tapped the microphone clipped to the podium, but of course it was dead, just like everything else in the world. He shuffled through the papers on top of the podium and found his handwritten notes for a sermon he'd never had the opportunity to give.

"You fixing to do some preaching, Reverend?"

Martin looked up, and saw John walking down the aisle. A moment later, Becky entered through the double doors, as well. The two of them took seats in the front row of pews.

"We figured we should come check on you," Becky said. "You've been up here all morning."

"Have I?" Martin frowned. He turned his wrist to look at his watch, and then remembered that it was back home on the nightstand. "I guess I have. Sorry about that. I must have lost track of time. Although you disappeared, as well, John."

"I was in the boiler room," the janitor explained.

"Is everything okay?"

"Oh, sure." John sounded surprised. "I was just messing around with stuff. You know? Trying to kick the boredom."

"I guess we're all growing restless," Martin agreed. "Maybe we should play some games or something. I believe there's a Scrabble board in the youth group room."

"That won't do me no good," John said. "On account of I ain't never learned to read too well. But you two can play and I'll watch. Maybe I'll pick up a thing or two."

"What's that?" Becky asked, nodding at the papers in Martin's hand.

"It was supposed to be my next sermon. Now, it's just words on paper."

"What was it about?"

Martin grinned humorlessly. "End time prophecy. The Rapture. The Tribulation period. Sort of ironic, isn't it?"

Becky nodded.

"The end of the world again." John sighed. "Ain't you preached about that before?"

"Sure," Martin said. "But it doesn't hurt to preach about it again. It's a big part of our faith, after all."

"I reckon so," John admitted. "The good book does talk about the dead coming back to life. I remember that. I just never thought it would be like this."

"I don't think what's happening outside is what the scripture was referring to," Martin said. "This is something else."

"I never thought I'd live to see the end of the world." Becky spoke quietly, and both men had to strain to hear her. "Do you two remember Lena Anderson?"

Martin and John nodded. Lena had been a member of the congregation for most of her life.

"She used to start every day and every night on her knees," Becky continued, "praying for the Rapture to occur. Terry Hamish told me that once, and I thought he was joking, but he wasn't. That really is how she lived her life. She spent

30

every day just waiting for the Rapture to happen."

"I reckon she was disappointed then," John said.

"To be fair," Martin told them, "Lena used her faith as a comfort. She lost her son in an automobile accident many years ago, and her faith in God was what got her through that terrible time. I think she just wanted to be reunited with her boy so badly that it manifested itself in the behavior you're talking about. It's a form of blind faith, but it's still faith. She got very mad at me once, years ago, when I mentioned that the Rapture itself is never referred to in the Bible."

"Can I be honest?" Becky asked. "The idea of the Rapture always scared me a little bit. Everyone disappearing in the blink of an eye—it scared me when I thought about what would happen to all those who got left behind. Think about the plane crashes and the wrecks on the highways, and folks laying on operating tables when their doctor vanishes. The world would be a scary place after that."

"It would indeed," Martin agreed.

"So why didn't it happen, then?" A single tear ran down Becky's cheek. "Why didn't we get called up to Heaven? The Rapture was supposed to happen before all this. It's supposed to happen before the Tribulation period, right?"

Martin nodded.

"Well, if it's the end of the world, then why are we still here?"

"Because it's not the end of the world," Martin said. "Not yet. As I said before, the things occurring outside have nothing to do with the Book of Revelation. This isn't the Tribulation period, Rebecca, nor is it the end of the world. God has plans for us. I firmly believe that. If I didn't, I'd collapse right now and curl into a ball and lose my mind. I'm not doing that because I believe that God has work for us to do. We just have to be patient until that plan is revealed to us."

John snorted. "No offense, Pastor, but I'm just about out of patience."

"I know you are, John. I know. I lose patience sometimes myself. I've prayed fervently every night, kneeling right down there at the railing, asking Him for deliverance. But so far, God hasn't seen fit to send an army of angels to smite our oppressors. He hasn't sent an earthquake or a tornado or the National Guard or any of the other things I've asked Him for. I've prayed for the power to come back on, or for a ham radio set, so that we'd know what's going on in the world, but He hasn't given us these things."

"He gave us a shotgun," John said. "I say we get on out of here and put it to use. If God isn't going to answer our prayers, then I reckon we ought to take matters into our own hands. It's like the Good Book says—God helps those who help themselves. Ain't that what you're always preaching?"

Not this again, Martin thought.

"Well?" John cocked his head, waiting. "Ain't it?"

Sighing, Martin stepped out from behind the podium and walked down to join them. Ignoring his flaring arthritis, he took a seat between them in the pew.

"Yes, John. God gave us a shotgun. He also gave us shelter and food and water and a place to sleep. He's kept us safe from those things outside. There are more and more of them every day. We all know they could break in here if they wanted to. But they haven't yet. Despite the odds, they haven't discovered us. And do you know why?"

John shook his head.

"Because God has protected us," Martin said. "He's protected us because He has plans for us. We must wait and follow His will."

"Well, I'm tired of waiting," John grumbled. "The way I see it, we're sitting ducks if we stay here. All this waiting around just increases our chances of being found out. Now, I've thought about it long and hard, and I've heard what you said, but my mind is made up. I've spent the morning getting things ready. Soon as it's dark outside, I'm leaving. I ain't asking either of you to come with me if you don't want to, but I expect you to respect my decision to leave. I ain't taking the shotgun or nothing with me. I reckon I can get to my place and get my own guns easy enough. Once I've got my truck, I'll swing back by here. If y'all have changed your minds, you can come with me. If not, then I'll just keep on driving and wish you luck."

"And where will you go?" Martin asked.

"I don't know, Reverend. Some place other than here, for starters. Fairlea and Lewisburg are close enough, I reckon. Maybe head on up over the river to Punkin Center. I've got friends on that side of the mountain. Teddy and Carl. Good ole' boys. They might have some ideas."

"I know Mr. Garnett and Mr. Seaton," Martin said. "We were in the same VFW chapter for a while. And I agree, if anyone could survive what's happening outside, it's the two of them. Teddy and Carl are a rare breed. But what if you don't make it that far, John? What if Lewisburg has been overrun?"

"Then I'll go the other way. Head out toward Clifton Forge or Hot Springs or Crow. Shoot on over the border into Virginia, or up towards Pennsylvania and Maryland. It don't matter none to me, long as it's someplace where this ain't happening."

"I don't think such a place exists anymore, John."

The janitor's eyes grew wet, and his voice was thick with emotion. "It has to, Pastor. It just has to. This can't be it. There has to be a safe zone out there somewhere. All I have to do is find it."

He's gone, Martin thought. *This is how his mind is coping with the stress of our situation. He's convinced himself that this safe zone exists, because he just can't fathom the alternative. There's no reasoning with him. Nothing Rebecca or I do or say will change his mind at this point, and I'm not sure I want to see what happens if we try.*

33

"You say it's God's will that you stay here," John whispered. "You say that the Lord has put it on your heart that you wait here for something. You don't know what that something is—"

"But I will when He reveals it to me," Martin interrupted.

"Well, that's just fine and dandy, Reverend. In the meantime, I reckon it's God's will that I leave. That's what He's put on my heart."

Martin took a deep breath and exhaled. His shoulder sagged. He suddenly felt very tired.

"Okay, John. If this is what you truly want, then I won't stand in your way. I just wish you'd reconsider. At the very least, sleep on it."

"I don't think I can sleep another night on these pews. They're killing my back."

Martin smiled sadly. "Fair enough."

John turned to Becky. "Will you come with me, or are you staying here? I got room in my truck. We might be able to get word to your loved ones, if we can find a safe zone."

"I'm staying." She looked at Martin as she answered, as if she were trying to convince him, too. "If the Reverend thinks this is where God wants us—that this is part of God's plan—then I'm inclined to believe him. He's never led our congregation wrong before."

"Congregation?" John pointed at the boarded-up windows. "What congregation? In case y'all haven't noticed, most of the folks who used to be a part of this congregation are now running around out there trying to eat everyone else."

"A congregation," Martin said, "is just like a church in that it's what you make it. We right here, the three of us, are a congregation. And you're right. Many of our fellow parishioners are out there, and it breaks my heart to see what they've become. I don't want to see you become one, too, John. That's why I'm asking you to stay. I don't want the same thing to happen to you. I don't want you to become one of them."

There was a moment of silence between the three of them. Martin felt something tickle his cheek. He reached up and brushed his face with his fingertips, and was surprised to find tears. He'd been unaware until then that he was crying. He wiped them away, his whiskers rough beneath his touch, and idly tried to remember how long it had been since he'd last shaved. Before the Rising, Martin had always made it a habit to shave every day, regardless of where he was or how he felt. Even when he was sick with the flu or camping in the woods, he'd made an effort to shave. His father had told him when he was younger—'shave every day and you'll feel better about yourself.' It was some of the best advice he'd ever been given, so simple and yet so true, and Martin had done his best to follow it every day. He glanced up, aware that John had been talking while he was reminiscing.

"I'm sorry. I was off in La-La Land there for a second. What were you saying?"

"I said that I appreciate it," John replied, his voice tinged with a mix of both conviction and regret, "but that my mind is made up. It's been made up since last night. But I don't want either of you to worry. I took care of everything this morning. The truth is, I wasn't just fooling around in the boiler room earlier. I moved the sewer grate and climbed down inside, just to make sure it was clear."

Becky gasped. "You had no right to do that, John! What if they had gotten inside?"

"They didn't get inside. I'm telling you, it's okay. I went down in the sewer and made sure everything was clear. There's nothing down there. I reckon they haven't figured out how to get in the sewers yet. Anyway, it's pretty much a straight shot from here to the end of the street. I can come out there, and then make my way to my place and get my truck. Once I find help, I'll come back. I promise."

Martin sighed. "We can't stop you, John. If you truly feel in your heart that you are meant to do this, then we won't stand in your way. But I'm begging you to reconsider. Please?"

"I can't, Pastor Martin. I don't know how to explain it to make you two understand. I'm not like you. I'm not good with words. But I can't stay here. I just…can't."

Martin nodded.

"Then may God go with you, John, for I have a feeling you'll need him."

***

They waited until nightfall, sharing one final, meager meal together—tomato soup, communion grape juice, and crackers. They ate in silence. None of them spoke because there was nothing left to say. John didn't ask for the shotgun and Martin didn't offer it to him. He considered it, but didn't voice it. Yes, the shotgun would benefit John on the outside, but if he actually managed to reach his home, he'd have access to other weapons. The same couldn't be said for Martin and Becky. Their defenses were limited to what they could improvise from the church's slim selection of tools.

When the meal was finished, Becky insisted on giving John some of the canned goods, but he politely declined.

"There's plenty of food in the pantry back at my place. I don't reckon I'll starve between here and there."

I don't reckon the zombies will, either, Martin thought. For a moment, he was concerned that he'd said it out loud, but when neither Becky nor John reacted, he relaxed.

"Have you considered what you'll do if you can't reach your home?" Martin asked.

"What do you mean?"

"Well, suppose you get halfway there and the zombies discover you. What happens then? What if you are cut off?"

John shrugged. "Then I'll find some other place to hide until the zombies leave. Don't worry, Pastor. I won't lead them back here."

"Oh, I wasn't worrying about that."

"You should be. I reckon I'd be worried about it if the roles were reversed."

"Perhaps," Martin said, "but I trust in the Lord. He'll keep us safe."

John nodded, but didn't respond.

As dusk turned to full darkness, they went to the windows and checked the peepholes one more time. A lone zombie shuffled by. Martin recognized the corpse as Mike Roden's son, Ben. Mike had been the manager at the White Sulphur Springs bank, and a member of the church. He'd served as lay speaker, and Ben, following in his father's footsteps, had volunteered several times as an acolyte. Martin remembered the boy in his white robe, lighting the altar candles at the beginning of Sunday services, and tried to contrast it with the dead thing outside. Ben was naked, except for a dirty, torn pair of underwear that hung halfway down his backside. One of his ears dangled over his shoulder on a thin strand of sinew. His back and legs were covered in ugly purple bite marks that leaked infection. The boy carried a skateboard at his side, as if he was planning on riding it if he found a suitable spot. Martin wondered if it was some sort of rudimentary instinct—a trace memory from before—or if the zombie really new how to use the skateboard? Martin had to resist the urge to call out to the boy. They watched quietly until Ben vanished from sight, and then waited another ten minutes. A black crow landed on a nearby tree. It took them a moment to determine that the bird was dead.

"Zombie birds," Becky said. "There goes the idea of putting a barrel on the roof to collect rainwater and bathe in."

John and Martin nodded without speaking. They watched the undead crow until it eventually flew away. Still, they waited, making sure no further zombies were in sight. Finally, John stirred, moving away from the window. His joints popped loudly in the silence.

"Looks like the coast is clear," he said. "If I'm gonna get going, I reckon now is the time."

"Are you sure?" Becky asked.

He nodded. "We've been over this. I'm sure. And like I said, I'll come back for y'all."

They walked downstairs and into the boiler room. Martin lit a candle so they could see. John selected a shovel from the tool rack on the wall and hefted it in his hands, testing its weight. Then he nodded, apparently satisfied.

"This will do. At least until I get to my place."

"Let us pray," Martin suggested.

Holding hands, the three of them stood in a circle over the sewer grate, closed their eyes and bowed their heads.

"Heavenly Father," Martin prayed, "we ask that you watch over our brother, John, and that You guard him with your grace and protection and the power of the Holy Spirit as he embarks on this journey. Lord, we cannot know Your mind, but John feels that You are speaking to his heart, and we ask that you continue to do so, no matter where the path before him might lead. We ask that he be filled with Your presence and Your love, and that he be bathed in the blood of the lamb, so that evil can not stand against him, and none may harm him. Lord, we ask that Your hand guide him, just as it has guided so many others, just as it guided Moses through the wasteland, and just as it wrote on the walls of the King's palace in the Book of Daniel. Safeguard our friend, that he may find what he's looking for and that he may do Your will. We ask these things in Your name. Amen."

"Amen," Becky and John echoed.

They released one another's hands and raised their heads. Martin tried to smile, but it felt fake. Instead, he patted John's shoulder and then squeezed.

"Go with God."

"Thank you, Reverend. I appreciate it. Got to be honest, I thought I'd be okay with this, but now I'm a little scared."

"You're changing your mind?" Martin tried to keep the hope from his voice.

"No, my mind is made up. Just afraid of what might happen. I ain't ever killed someone before. I mean, I've hunted all my life. Killed plenty of deer and squirrels and wild turkeys. Even just a black bear up on Bald Knob about twelve years ago. But killing a person is different. Hopefully, I won't have to."

"They're not people anymore," Becky said. "Keep that in mind. They're dead."

"Dead or alive, they're still people. Right, Reverend?"

"I don't know," Martin admitted. "I wish I did, but I just don't know."

Wiping the sweat from his forehead with the back of his hand, John then looped a length of thick steel chain through the bars of the sewer grate. He squatted on his haunches and gripped the chain with both hands. Then, grunting, he pulled on the chain until the grate came free. Martin was surprised by how easily it moved, until he remembered that John had been in the boiler room earlier, preparing the way. The grating slid across the cement floor, scraping it, and clanged as he moved it aside. Panting, he looked up at both of them, and wiped his forehead again.

"Y'all think you can move this back into place after I'm gone?"

"I reckon so," Martin said. "Between the two of us, I'm sure we can drag it back over the hole. I'm not so sure we'll be able to lift it again, though, once it's back in place."

"Well, then let's hope you don't need to."

"Exactly."

John sat down on the floor and swung his legs over the shaft. Then he lowered the shovel down into the hole. Martin and Becky heard the spade strike bottom. Then John pulled a small flashlight from his pocket and turned it on. The beam made his face seem ghostly. He stared at them both.

"Good luck, John," Martin said. "May the Lord bless you and keep you and watch over you."

"Thanks again, Reverend."

Becky leaned forward and gave John a quick kiss on the top of his head. He blushed.

"For luck," she said. "That's all."

"Can I get another one for extra luck?"

"Now you're pushing your luck, John, and wasting the luck I just gave you."

Martin chuckled. Then Rebecca did the same. John looked at them both and grinned. Then his expression grew serious again.

"I promise y'all that I'll come back. Just as soon as I find help, I'll come back for you both. I mean it."

Martin nodded. "We'll be here, God willing."

John shook his hand again. Then, without another word, he lowered himself into the shaft. It was only about seven feet deep, but it seemed to Martin that the floor swallowed him up. His flashlight beam was barely imperceptible at the bottom. They hovered over the hole, watching as John crept forward into the sewer tunnel. Soon, both his footsteps and his flashlight beam faded.

"Let's go watch," Becky said. "The very least we can do is see him off properly."

"Okay." He didn't voice his fear that they might be about to witness their friend's death.

They returned upstairs and resumed their positions at the peepholes. They watched the spot where John had indicated the sewer emerged. For what seemed like a very long time, nothing happened. Then, Martin saw movement. John crawled up out of the ground and cautiously glanced around. Then he collected his shovel, turned toward the church and offered a quick wave. Martin waved back, knowing full well that there was no way John could see them through the plywood, but doing so anyway. John gave one last glance over his shoulder. After that, he was gone, slipping into the darkness. They watched until he vanished from sight.

"Do you think we'll ever see him again?" Becky asked.

"John's a man of his word. He said he'd come back. If it is the Lord's will, then yes, I think we'll see him again."

Much later, Martin would reflect that God must have had other plans, because neither he nor Rebecca ever saw John Amos Kuhn again.

THREE

The serpent entered their sanctuary just after breakfast the next morning. Their day started late, as both Martin and Becky had overslept. Martin had awoken in the middle of the night and heard Becky crying softly. As he lay there in the darkness, trying to wake up enough to go to her, he realized that she was trying to stifle the sound. Her sobs were muffled, but the pew trembled slightly as she wept. He'd stayed where he was, trying to decide if he should go to her or respect her privacy. Eventually, he called her name, and the sounds ceased.

After a moment, Becky had apologized for waking him, and he told her it was okay, and then he went to her. They sat up for a while, talking of the world they'd left behind, and of all the people and things that had died with it. They remembered movies and television programs and the last book they'd read and favorite places to go, and how none of those things were there anymore. There would be no new movies or television shows or books, and all of their favorite places were now overrun with zombies. Eventually. Becky had fallen asleep with her head on Martin's shoulder. When he awoke, his arm, which had been wrapped around her all night, was numb and stiff. He knew that his arthritis would be bad for the rest of the day.

Becky woke with a start, bolting upright and gasping when she realized what had happened. They'd quickly disentangled, mumbling embarrassed apologies to each other.

"You shouldn't have let me sleep so long," she said, blushing.

"I reckon we both needed it."

Becky hurried downstairs while Martin checked the perimeter. He brushed at his collar as he went to the window. It was still damp with either Becky's saliva or her tears—or maybe both.

He looked outside. The dead were up with the sun. A half dozen of them milled around outside the church, wandering through the street and the field. He could smell them this morning—the thick, almost overwhelming stink of rotting meat. He wondered if the stench was stronger because their decomposition was advancing, or if it was something as simple as a change in the direction of the wind.

The zombie crow—or another just like it—was back, and this time, it had brought friends. The flock, six birds strong, attacked a sparrow, pecking the smaller bird to death. Martin grimaced as they tore strips of flesh from its body with their beaks. After a few minutes, what was left of the sparrow began to move again. Then it joined the others.

"Even the smallest creatures are not safe from this evil, my Lord. What chance do we have, save by Your grace and mercy?"

As he watched, Martin was alarmed to see several of the zombies enter a few of the vacant homes. They smashed down doors and broke through windows. Finding no one to devour, they soon emerged back onto the street. Once again, none of them showed any interest in the church, and Martin breathed a prayer of thanks to God for keeping him and Rebecca safe. Eventually, the zombies moved on, in search of prey.

After washing up with a sanitary wipe, Martin joined Becky in the kitchen. He noticed that she seemed happier—more talkative. When she served him his meal, she touched his shoulder and when she passed him the salt, her fingertips lingered on the back of his hand.

"Thank you for last night," she said. "I'm sorry about—"

"It's okay. It's my job, to comfort folks when they are depressed or grieving or feeling forlorn."

"Oh…yes, of course it is. Well, I appreciate it, Reverend. It meant a lot."

"It was my pleasure."

"I… I don't know what I'd do without you. You've been a great comfort to me. You're like a rock. I thank God you're here. And I thank you, too."

"You don't have to thank me. Seriously. We're in this together, Rebecca, and with God's help, we'll get through."

She leaned closer, staring intently into his eyes. Martin noticed that her lips were parted. They shone in the dim light, wet and full. Her teeth were very white. Despite the heat in the stuffy kitchen, Martin shivered

Chesya, he thought. *I miss you, darling. How long has it been? Give me strength, Lord.*

Becky cleared her throat and stood. She moved too quickly and her chair tipped over and hit the tiles with a bang. They both froze for a moment, wondering if the sound could be heard by the dead. When there was no uproar from outside, they both laughed, breaking the tension.

"I'll…uh…" Martin wiped his hands on his shirt. "I'll be right back. Let me just double check the perimeter."

"We'll be okay." Becky avoided meeting his eye, focusing instead on clearing away their paper plates. "Like you said, God is watching over us."

"Too true, but God also helps those who help themselves."

Becky smiled. "Well, like I said, I feel safe here with you."

Martin felt his pulse quicken as he hurried out of the kitchen and into the Sunday School rooms. He walked by the closed door to the boiler room and thought of John—and that was when he saw the snake. It was wriggling out from under the crack in the boiler room door. He identified it from the shape of its head and its color and markings as a copperhead.

Probably a young one, judging from its narrow and thin size.

He backed away from the door, and bumped his shin on a bookshelf filled with inspirational literature. Martin had never liked snakes, especially poisonous ones, and especially copperheads. At least rattlesnakes and cobras had the good manners to warn you before they attacked. Not so a copperhead. They struck silent and deadly. As he watched, the serpent slithered into the room, raised its head, and stared at him. Its tongue flicked the air, as if tasting it. The snake lowered its head again and made a beeline toward him.

Martin took a deep breath. He was about to shout a warning to Becky, and then he smelled it—that same rank stink of decay that he'd smelled wafting from the zombies outside. He glanced back down at the snake and realized that it was the source of the stench. Now that it was closer, he realized that much of its skin was missing. Tiny vertebrae protruded from the wounds.

"Oh Lord," he moaned. "Oh my dear Lord. Get thee behind me, serpent."

The snake wriggled faster, hissing as it drew near. As had happened with the zombie dog pack, Martin was reminded of speech. He backed up into the wall, fists clenched as the snake came within striking distance. His left arm began to tingle, as if asleep. Martin flexed his fingers and frowned. A dull pain throbbed in his chest, and slowly began to grow stronger.

A heart attack, Lord? Come on. Not now!

The pain subsided and Martin turned his attention back to his attacker. The creature raised its head again and darted forward, striking at his ankle, but Martin was quicker. Ignoring both the lingering discomfort in his chest and the arthritic aching in his joints, he leaped into the air. The snake missed. A second later, Martin landed on its pointed head with both feet. The tiny skull crunched beneath the heels of his boots. The serpent's tail twitched once, and then was still.

"The serpent thou shalt trample under feet. That's from the Book of Psalms, you son of a bitch."

He ground his feet back and forth, crushing the snake against the tile floor. Blood trickled out from under his boots. Satisfied, Martin stepped away and examined the corpse, making sure that it was dead again. After determining that it wouldn't be crawling ever again, he hurried toward the kitchen, leaving bloody foot-prints in his wake.

"Thank you Lord," he prayed aloud. "Thank you for helping me to defeat your old foe. I appreciate the strength in the face of adversity. And if you could, Lord, please don't let any more of those things inside. I think the snake was creepier than any of the ones out there."

Becky poked her head out of the kitchen. "Did you say something, Thomas?"

Martin was shaken by his encounter with the zombie, but not enough that he wasn't surprised to hear the organist refer to him by his first name. He didn't mind, but it seemed sudden and shocking, after years of her referring to him as Reverend or Pastor. Perhaps Becky noticed the effect it had on him, because when she spoke again, she returned to the old familiar standby.

"Reverend Martin? What's wrong? You look like you've seen a ghost."

"Not a ghost," Martin panted. "A zombie."

"Where? Outside?"

He shook his head. "No. In here. Right over there."

"They got in? Oh, God…"

"Don't worry. I killed it…well, if you can truly call it that. I mean, how do you kill something that's already dead? But never mind the semantics. It's right over here. No need to worry. It's harmless now. I…" He paused, swallowing. "I'm sorry. I'm rambling, aren't I?"

"It's okay. But are the doors and windows secure? Are there more inside the church?"

He shook his head. "I don't think so. It was just the one."

"Do we…did we know them?"

Martin led her across the room and pointed at the smashed snake. "I don't think this one was a member of our church."

Gasping, Becky backed away from the corpse. "A copperhead! Oh, Reverend, what if there are more? I won't be able to sleep tonight knowing there are snakes in here."

"I don't think there are, Becky. This one was dead already. I think it came in from the sewer. Maybe it saw John leave, or maybe it discovered the tunnel after he was gone, but I think it had a very specific purpose. And I've no doubt that it would have killed me or somehow alerted the other zombies to our presence, if I hadn't destroyed it."

"Are you sure?"

"Ninety-nine point nine percent. If there were more of them in the church, I reckon they would have attacked us by now."

"So what do we do?"

"Let's check the boiler room. We should figure out some way to seal off that sewer grate. Then I'll double check all the fortifications. Make sure everything is still sealed up tight."

Becky's lower lip trembled and her eyes were wide. She glanced back down at the snake and then up at him. Martin took her by the shoulders and pulled her close. Once again, the smell of her hair was intoxicating. He took a deep breath.

"We'll be okay. I promise. The Lord has looked after us so far. He's not going to abandon us now."

She nodded against his chest. For a moment, Martin wanted to stay like that, just standing there with her pressed tight against him, feeling her warmth, the smoothness of her skin beneath his fingertips, her scent filling his nose, her very proximity intoxicating him, stirring up long-buried emotions and de-sires.

And then he thought of Chesya again, and those feelings vanished, replaced with a sharp pang of regret. He missed her. Even now, he missed his wife. And what he was doing wasn't right. It wasn't right for him and it wasn't fair to Rebecca. He wasn't emotionally available. He'd known it the other night, when they'd been upstairs, and he was reminded of it again now. Filled with regret, he pushed himself away from Becky and held her at arm's length.

"We should check the boiler room, before any more of them do manage to get in."

She nodded. "Okay."

They crossed the Sunday School rooms. Becky reached out and took his hand. Her palm was damp with sweat. She squeezed his fingers. Martin squeezed back, trying to ease her fears. Then he let go of her hand and opened the door.

The boiler room was dark and chilly and smelled of mildew and motor oil. Martin much preferred those odors over the stench of the dead. Since the room was free of that, he assumed that no more zombies had discovered the sewer. Still, he was unnerved as he checked the corners and crannies for more zombie snakes, rats or anything else that could have squeezed through the grate. Becky stood by the door, holding it open. When Martin was finished searching, he moved over to the grate and stared down into the shaft. It was pitch black at the bottom, but he saw nothing moving in the shadows. The only sound was a faint trickle of water far below.

He looked around and saw a pile of lawn fertilizer bags stacked against one wall. Martin placed a sheet of plywood down over the grate and then, with some difficulty due to his arthritis, moved the fertilizer bags on top of it. By the time he was done, his face was lathered in sweat and he was panting hard. His chest gave a few quick pains, but there was no flare-up like before.

"Whew." He wiped his forehead with the back of his hand. "That should do the trick."

"I hope so," Becky said. "What if one of the human

zombies comes through the tunnel, though?"

"I don't think they can get enough leverage from the bottom of the shaft. But I'll tell you what. Just in case, maybe we should make some kind of early warning system."

"Like what?"

Martin moved over to the tool bench and picked up a coffee can full of nails, screws and other miscellaneous bits. He sat it on top of the fertilizer bags, and then added some aerosol cans and other junk. Then he stood back and admired his handiwork.

"There. Now if any of them do manage to push through the blockade, we'll hear them coming when all of this crashes to the floor. Feel better about things?"

"Yes, I do. Thank you, Thomas. I'm just…like I said before, I don't know what I'd do without you here. You must be thirsty. Let me get you something to drink."

He nodded, too unsure of his own emotions to respond, not knowing what he'd say if he tried.

***

Dinner that night was something special—a vegetable stew Becky made from cans of corn, green beans, peas, diced tomatoes, carrots, chick peas and beef broth. When Martin swirled his plastic spoon around the bowl and saw the bounty, he was surprised.

"Becky, are you sure that you should have used all this? Shouldn't we be rationing our canned goods?"

"This is a special occasion."

"It is?"

"Sure, it is. You killed a zombie today. Kept us safe."

Martin grinned. "It wasn't much, really. To be honest, I was terrified. Thought for sure I was going to have a heart attack there for a moment."

"You did fine. I thought I'd repay your bravery with

something other than canned tomato soup and communion wafers."

"Well, I do appreciate it, Rebecca." He spooned a mouthful and groaned with delight. "It's delicious."

"Good. I'm glad you like it."

"Oh, I do. I'm just worried about our supplies. Are you certain we have enough to last? And what will we do with the leftover soup? We can't refrigerate it."

"We have plenty. And we've been starving ourselves. I don't think there will be any leftovers tonight."

Martin's smile broadened. "Gluttony is a sin."

Becky returned his smile. "So are a lot of things."

***

She came to him that night after he'd fallen asleep. He awoke to the sounds of her stirring, of cloth on skin. Her pew creaked and groaned when she stood up. She was nude. Even in the darkness, Martin could tell that. And when she took his trembling hand and placed it on her breast, he felt it, as well. Her nipple stiffened beneath his fingers, and she moaned softly.

"Becky... Rebecca... I..."

"Make love to me, Thomas. Please?"

"Becky..."

He pulled his hand away and she flinched. Martin sat up in the pew and turned away. She reached for him, cupped his chin in her hand, and turned him back toward her.

"What's wrong, Thomas?"

"We can't. I can't. It's not right."

"It's not wrong, either. We don't need to talk about it, Thomas. It doesn't even need to mean anything. But I'm scared and I'm lonely and I'm cold, and I need to feel something. I need to feel somebody. I need to feel loved, and wanted. And safe. If only for a little while. Please?"

"Rebecca, listen to me. It's not that I don't find you attractive, and it's not that I don't want you. Believe me, I've thought about it. The Lord knows that."

"Is that it? Your faith? Martin, God won't care. He knows that it's right."

"No, Rebecca. It's not right."

"I'll beg, if you want me to. Please, Thomas. We don't know what's going to happen tomorrow. The zombies could figure out we're inside here and break in. We could run out of food. You said you almost had a heart attack today. We don't know what will happen."

"But we don't know what will happen tomorrow anyway, Rebecca. It doesn't take the end of the world to feel that way. Life is uncertainty. That's why it's important to be strong in your faith. We can be gone in an instant."

"Do you think I don't know that?" Her breasts jiggled as she talked. Martin couldn't help but look at them. Something stirred in his gut.

"Everyone we know and love is dead," Becky continued, "or worse, they're one of those things outside. Everything and everyone is gone. Our friends. Our family members. And now John is gone, too, and it's just us. We're alone here, and we could be next. You could be gone tomorrow. I could be, too. I don't want to die, Thomas. I want to live. I want to feel alive. Make me feel alive. Make me feel good, even if just for a little while. Please do this for me?"

She moved closer, leaning toward him. Her nipples brushed against his whiskered cheek. Groaning, Martin turned away. He felt himself stiffen, even as his eyes filled with tears. Becky reached down, grabbed his wrist, and before Martin was aware of what was happening, she guided his hand between her legs. Martin sighed. She was slick and warm there, and her wetness dribbled down the inside of her thighs and across his fingers.

"I can't," he moaned. He tried to pull his hand away, but

his body resisted. "Please stop this, Rebecca. Please don't do this to me."

"Why not? What's so wrong with me? I don't understand."

"It's not you. It's me."

She tried to guide his fingers to her swollen clitoris, but Martin yanked free, and clutched his wrist as if he'd been burned. Rebecca glared at him as if she'd been slapped.

"It's not you, it's me? You're really going to use that old cliché, Thomas?"

"It's true. It's not that I don't find you desirable, Rebecca. I do. I meant what I said. You're a beautiful woman, and any man would be lucky to have you as his wife. But that's just it. I already have a wife. I'm married."

Her brow furrowed in confusion. "Chesya? But she's... Martin, she's been gone how many years now?"

"I know. And I know that I should move on. You're not the first person who has told me that. But in my heart, we're still married. I still love her. Believe me, I'd like to move on. I'd like to find deliverance—to be able to live and love again. But I can't. When I'm with you, I think of her. I just miss her so much. I've asked the Lord to give me something to take her off my mind. I've prayed for a new task that I might focus on, but none is forthcoming. I want to be with her, and I can't. It's not fair!"

His tears flowed freely then. Martin tried to say more, tried to explain, but his words were lost in sobs.

Becky said nothing. She stood over him, watching him cry. She reached out a tentative hand, but Martin waved her away. After a few minutes, she returned to her pew and got dressed in silence. Then she returned.

"It's okay, Reverend. I understand, and I'm sorry."

Sniffling, Martin wiped his nose with his sleeve. He noticed that she was back to calling him by his title rather than his name.

"Don't be sorry, Becky. I'm the one who should be

apologizing."

"No, don't you dare. This was my fault. I had no right. I just…I thought you felt the same way."

"I wish I could," Martin whispered. "You don't know how much I wish that."

Becky smiled at him, but her mouth was tight and the gesture wasn't reflected in her eyes.

"It's okay," she said again. "We don't have to talk about it anymore. I'll sleep downstairs tonight."

"Are you sure? You don't have to—"

"I want to. I need to. You're hurting, Martin, but I'm hurting too."

"I'm sorry."

"Don't be. It's all right. I'll be okay. I just need some time to myself. Okay?"

"Okay."

"I'll see you in the morning."

Martin nodded. "Yes. I'll see you then. We can talk more about it at breakfast, if you like."

"There's nothing more to say," Becky reassured him. "I'll be okay. I will. Just give me a little space. Tomorrow is another day. Good night, Martin."

"Good night, Rebecca. I'll see you in the morning."

***

The next morning, when Martin awoke, Becky was gone. An investigation of the boiler room showed that she'd moved the blockade aside and gone out the same way John had. She left a note in the kitchen, and had placed the jar of instant coffee on top of it to insure that Martin would find it. He picked up the paper with shaking hands, and read it.

Dear Reverend Martin,

I'm sorry again about what happened tonight. I didn't mean to do that to you. I didn't know. But I do now, and I understand. Chesya was a lucky woman to have you in her life. She was lucky to have a man who loved her the way you still do. It occurs to me that maybe she's lucky in other ways, too. She died before any of this happened, so she didn't end up like everyone else who has died. Perhaps that was God's will? Maybe he spared her from that fate by taking her home early, before everything fell apart. It's like you always say, we can't guess the mind of God.

I know that you feel that it's the Lord's will that we stay here. I believe that you believe this to be true. But I also know that I have to listen to my own heart and my own head, and hope that what I'm feeling is God making His will known to me. Because what I'm feeling right now is heartbreak. I need to leave this place. I can't stay here anymore. Not after what just happened. We'd always have that hanging in the air between us, and even if it remained unspoken, it would still be there. Eventually, it would poison us, and I don't want that to happen. I want you to have a clear conscience, so that when God does reveal your deliverance from this place, you are clear-headed enough to know it.

I took some of the food and water. Just

enough to get me by until I find some more.
I'm leaving the shotgun. I don't know how
to use it, anyway. I'm taking the pick-axe
from the boiler room.

Don't look for me, Thomas. Don't come
outside. If you truly believe that God wants
you to wait here, then please don't let
me jeopardize that. I couldn't bear it if I
made you doubt the will of the Lord, on top
of the hurt I've already caused you. And
don't worry about me. I'll be okay. Yes, I
know very well what will probably happen
to me out there, but I also know that it
won't matter, because I'll be with God. Our
friends and loved ones will be there, too.
So will Chesya. We'll all be waiting for you.

Love,
Rebecca

Sighing, Martin read it again, letting the words sink in. Then, crumpling the note into a ball, he cast it aside and screamed.

"Why have you forsaken me, Lord? Why have you let this happen? First John, and now Rebecca. What do you want of me? What am I waiting for? What is it that you want me to do? I have prayed and begged for deliverance, and yet you stay silent. You never talk to me! Why me, Lord? Please, please give me an answer. Let me know your will. Please…"

His cries faded. Grief-stricken, Martin ran out of the kitchen and dashed up the stairs, taking them two at a time. He went to the peephole, knowing it was already too late, but looking anyway. He wept at what he saw.

Rebecca was gone.

The dead were not. They milled about, wandering in and

out of his view. Martin watched them, blinking away tears and trying to stifle his sobs. Gradually, he became aware of a far-off droning sound. As it drew nearer, he realized what it was.

An airplane. He wondered who was in it and where they were coming from, and where they were going. Who were these hardy survivors and how had they managed to commandeer an air-plane? Then he realized that their identity and story wasn't important. What mattered was that they were alive.

Somewhere overhead, life went on.

And somewhere above that, his loved ones were waiting for him.

FOUR

Martin stared at Jesus on the cross and thought about resurrection.

Lazarus had lain dead in his tomb for four days before Jesus came along. Martin opened his Scofield Reference Bible and turned to the Book of John. In Chapter 11, Verse 39, Martha told Jesus "by this time he stinketh; for he hath been dead four days."

That was pretty specific.

So was the account of Jesus bringing Lazarus back from the dead. "Lazarus come forth!" and the dead man did just that, still bound in grave clothes. Jesus then commanded the crowd to turn Lazarus loose, after which John dropped the narrative and moved on to the conversion of the Jews and the Pharisee conspiracy.

Nowhere in the Bible did it say Lazarus went around eating people.

The Bible that Martin had known, taught, and loved for the last forty years was full of examples of the dead coming back to life. But not like this.

"He that believes in me shall have eternal life," Martin spoke aloud. His voice sounded very small in the empty church. He wondered again if the things he had glimpsed in the street were still believers.

John and Rebecca had been gone for two weeks. As he'd done every day since they'd departed, he prayed for their safety and for their souls. He wondered where they were now. Were they alive out there, in some new sanctuary free of a crazy old preacher who was so afraid to move on or go outside that he'd convinced himself—and almost convinced them—that it was God's will that they sit here and starve to death? Or were they dead, their souls in Heaven and their bodies commandeered by demons from the Pit? And if so, would the zombie version of them come back here looking for him?

Filled with despair, Martin moved across the church to the boarded-over stained glass windows and peered through a knothole in the plywood.

And then he got an answer to his question.

Though not quite dawn, the darkness was already receding. Becky had finally returned. She had lost her dress. Now, she squatted among the shrubs, clad only in a filthy pair of once-white cotton panties. Martin closed his eyes, remembering how she'd felt against his skin, remembering her warmth and wetness. Those things were gone now, and this was a perversion of the woman who had loved him. Her sagging breasts swayed freely.

"Oh, Rebecca. I am so sorry. Please forgive me."

She gnawed on a human forearm as if it were a chicken leg, and then cast it aside, staring off into the distance and moaning softly. Something had attracted her attention. Martin strained, trying to see what she was looking at.

A man appeared, cautiously limping down the street. His jeans and flannel shirt were dirty and torn. He clutched a pistol, but the weapon dangled limply by his side. He did not seem to notice the corpse moving in the shadows. Wearily, he collapsed to his knees on the sidewalk. The hedges rustled and Becky darted forward. Half-conscious, the man seemed unaware of the impending danger.

"Hey," Martin shouted, beating his fists against the plywood. "Look out!"

Mouthing a quick prayer, he dashed into the narthex and struggled to move the heavy wooden pew propped against the door. For a brief moment, he considered exiting the church through the sewer tunnel, but that would take too long, and the man would be dead by the time he got outside. Sliding the pew aside, Martin grabbed the shotgun from the coat rack, undid the four recently installed deadbolts, and ran out into the street.

"Heads up," Martin yelled. "Behind you!"

Hearing the commotion, the stranger turned as the zombie lurched toward him. He raised the pistol and fired. The bullet tore through Becky's shoulder. Running across the yard, Martin ducked as the second shot missed its mark completely.

"Don't shoot me," he cried. "I'm not one of them."

The man squeezed the trigger again, and missed once more. He fired a fourth time, but the clip was empty. Confused, he looked at the pistol, and then stared up at Becky.

She squealed with delight, and Martin shivered at the sound. Becky reached for her victim.

The man closed his eyes, and Martin heard him whisper, "I'm sorry, Danny."

Martin slammed the shotgun into the creature's back. Becky toppled face first to the sidewalk. Her now-yellowed teeth shattered on the pavement. Martin jacked a shotgun shell into the chamber, and placed the barrel against the base of the zombie's skull. Becky screamed in rage.

"Go with God, Rebecca."

He squeezed the trigger. Brain matter and skull fragments sprayed across the sidewalk like a Rorschach pattern. Martin closed his eyes, but it was too late. The image had already burned into his brain. The sun peeked over the rooftops and the roar of the shotgun echoed through the quiet streets, greeting the dawn.

I'm sorry, Martin thought. *I'm so sorry...*

He turned to the new arrival. "I'm afraid that's going to attract attention. We'd best get inside."

He held his hand out to the man, and the stranger took it. His grip was firm and his hands bore the calluses of a working man—possibly a farmer or mechanic or construction worker. Martin had shaken many hands over the years, as he greeted each parishioner after the sermon. He'd become a good judge of what a man did for a living just by the texture of their palms.

"Thank you, Father," the man said.

"Pastor, actually," Martin corrected him, smiling. "Reverend Thomas Martin. And there's no need to thank me. Give your thanks to the Lord after we're safe."

"Jim Thurmond, and yeah, let's get off the street."

A hungry cry, followed by another, was all the incentive they needed.

Well, Martin thought. *They know I'm here now. Just a matter of time before they find my hiding place.*

"Is this your church, Reverend?"

Martin smiled again. "It's God's church. I just work here."

***

Martin fixed Jim a makeshift bed using blankets and a pew. He tried not to think about the fact that it was the pew where Becky had slept, and that it was her blankets that the new arrival was now using. He tried to remember the sound of her voice, and was alarmed to find that he couldn't. Desperate, he tried to remember how she had felt that last night, but the only image that came to mind was her head exploding.

Jim resisted Martin's efforts, insisting that he only needed to rest for a moment. Then he promptly fell into a deep but troubled sleep. Martin sipped instant coffee and stood watch over him, listening to the occasional shriek of the things outside.

Shortly before noon, a wandering zombie discovered Becky's corpse and began to feed on her remains. Martin watched in revulsion as, like ants, more of the creatures emerged, attracted to the feast. Occasionally, the zombies glanced around at the surrounding houses and the church. Martin wondered if they would finally be moved to investigate his sanctuary, but they seemed satisfied with the free lunch. An hour later, when the knot of fetid things had finally scattered, nothing remained of Becky except bones and a few red bits, smeared across the sidewalk and grass.

***

Jim awoke at sundown, alarmed at first. His expression was frantic. He sat up, looking around the church in panic. Martin smiled at him in the candlelight, trying to project calmness and reassurance.

"Here you go." Martin handed him a steaming cup of coffee that he'd just heated downstairs. "It's not very good, but I reckon it'll wake you up."

"Thanks," Jim nodded. He sipped it and took in the surroundings. "Pretty secure. You do all these fortifications yourself?"

Martin laughed softly. "Yes, by the grace of God, but not by myself. We managed to get the place squared away before it got bad. I had some help. John, our janitor and handyman—the church caretaker. He's the one who got the windows boarded over."

"Where is he now?"

Martin's expression clouded. He didn't speak for a moment.

"I don't know," he said finally. "Dead I suppose. Or undead, more likely. He left two weeks ago. Insisted on getting his pickup truck. He'd planned on driving us out of here. He was convinced that this was a localized problem, and thought the government might have this section of the state cordoned off. He thought there had to be a safe zone out there. Some place where this wasn't happening. John figured we should make for Beckley or Lewisburg, or maybe Richmond. I never saw him again."

"It's like this everywhere, as far as I can tell," Jim told him. "I—I came from Lewisburg."

"On foot too, it would seem," Martin commented in wonderment. "How did you manage that?"

"I almost didn't," Jim admitted. "I was on auto-pilot, I guess."

"These are times when men are forced to do what they must." Martin sighed. "I had hoped that maybe John was right. That maybe it was different elsewhere. I prayed for a ham radio set, or even a decent pair of those AM/FM headphones I see the kids wearing, just so I could know what was happening. I've had no contact with folks, and the power has pretty much been out, except for a few streetlights here and there. I heard a plane go overhead a few days ago, but that's been it."

"The power was still on in Lewisburg—or at least it was when I left. I had radio, TV, and the internet. They're worthless though. There's nothing—no one. As for this being a localized event, it's been going on over a month. I think they'd have had troops in here by now, if that was the case."

Martin thought about this, then excused himself and disappeared into the side room next to the altar. Normally, it was where the acolyte, scripture reader and lay speaker sat before the service began. Since John and Rebecca's departure, Martin had been using it to store food and water, so that he wouldn't have to go downstairs as much. Going downstairs and eating breakfast in the church kitchen filled him with loneliness.

Returning, Martin offered Jim a meal of Oreo cookies, bread, animal crackers, and warm grape juice for dinner.

"I got the cookies and crackers from the Sunday School room," he explained. "The bread and juice were for supposed to be for communion, but I don't think the Lord will mind."

They ate in silence. After a few minutes, Martin caught Jim staring at him.

"Why?" Jim asked.

"Why what?"

"Why did God let this happen? I thought the end of the world was supposed to be when Russia invaded Israel and you couldn't buy anything without having a 666 on your credit card."

"That's one interpretation," Martin said. "But you're talking about end-time prophecy and you've got to remember, there are many, many different ideas about what it all means."

"I thought that when the Rapture happened, the dead would return to life? Isn't that what's happening now?"

"Well, the actual word 'Rapture' never occurs in the Old or New Testament. That came along much later. But yes, the Bible does speak of the dead returning to life, after a fashion, to live with the Lord upon his return."

"No offense Reverend, but if He's returned, then He's made a hell of a mess of things."

"But that's just it, Jim. The Lord hasn't returned—at least, not yet. What's happening isn't of God. It's of Satan, who was given mastery over the Earth. Yet even in this, we must stand firm and trust in the will of the Lord."

"Do you believe that, Reverend Martin? Do you really believe that this is God's will?"

Martin paused, choosing his words carefully.

"If you're asking me if I believe in God, Jim, then yes. Yes I do. But more importantly, I believe that there is a reason for everything, good and bad. Despite what you may have heard, bad things are not caused by God. When there's a tornado, that isn't God's will. But it's his love and power that gives us the strength to carry on in the tornado's wake, and it's that same love that will get us through now. I believe we have been spared for a reason."

But do I really believe that? Martin thought. *Is there really a reason we've been spared? Do I dare believe it anymore? I've sat here, waiting for deliverance, waiting for God to show me what He wants me to do, and look at what its cost. Have I been a fool all this time?*

"I have a reason, alright." Jim nodded, standing. "My son is alive, and I've got to make it to New Jersey and save him. Thanks for the meal and the shelter, Reverend, and more importantly, thanks for saving my ass today. I'd like to pay you, if you'll let me. I don't have much, but I've got some extra sardines and Tylenol in my pack—"

"Your son is alive?" Martin repeated. "How can you be sure? New Jersey is a long way off."

"He called me last night on my cell phone."

Martin stared at Jim, unable to speak. Something stirred deep inside of him. For the first time since Rebecca's departure, he felt hope.

"I know it sounds crazy," Jim said, "but it happened! He's alive and hiding out in my ex-wife's attic. I'm got to get to him."

Slowly, Martin rose from the pew.

"Then I'll help you."

"Thanks Martin. Really, thanks. But I can't ask you to do that. I need to move quickly, and I don't want—"

"Nonsense," Martin interrupted. "You asked me about God's will and the meaning in all of this. Well, it's His will that you received that call, and it's His will that kept you alive to receive it. And it's also His will that I help you."

"I can't ask you to do that."

"You're not asking me. God is." Martin stamped his foot, then more quietly, said, "I feel this in my heart."

Jim stared at him, unflinching. Then, slowly, a grin spread across his tired face.

"All right." He reached out a hand. "If it is God's will

and everything, I guess I can't stand in the way of that."

They shook hands, and sat back down.

"So what's your plan?" Martin asked.

"We need a vehicle. I don't reckon the church has one that we could use?"

"No," Martin shook his head. "That's why John left. To get his truck. But there's plenty in the streets and driveways."

"I don't suppose a man of the cloth knows how to hotwire one?"

"No, but there's a dealership just off the interstate. We could get one there, keys and everything. It sits right off Interstate Sixty-Four. The lights were still on there, last time I checked. You can see the lights at night on the horizon."

"Works for me," Jim said, mulling it over. "When can we make a move? I can't waste any more time."

"We'll leave tonight," Martin said. "Those things don't really sleep, but the darkness will give us more cover. That's how I've avoided discovery so far. I stay quiet, watch for them during the day, and sleep at night. With the boards over the windows, they can't spot the candlelight, and I've been careful not to give them a reason to be curious."

"Well, let's hope that luck holds."

"I told you, Jim. It's not luck—it's God. All you have to do is ask Him."

Jim began reloading his pistol. "In that case Pastor Martin, I'm going to ask for an armored tank."

Martin smiled, thinking about prayers, and how God always answered them, eventually. Sometimes, the answer wasn't what you expected, or even wanted, but you got an answer all the same. All one had to do was wait for it. Perhaps Jim would indeed get his tank before this was through. Martin would pray for that, as well. When Jim spoke of his son, Martin was reminded of Mark and William. There was nothing greater than a father's love for his children, because it was in that love that hope sprang eternal.

Jim remained focused on his weapon. Martin left him to his thoughts and bowed his head.

Thank you for my deliverance, Lord. I see now why You had me wait here and what it is You would have me do, and I am grateful and honored for the task. Your will be done, on Earth as it is in Heaven. And if it pleases You, Father, answer this man's prayers, as well. Let us find his son, happy and healthy, and let the two of them be reunited and find a deliverance of their own.

AFTERWORD

For a guy who keeps swearing that he's done with zombies, I sure do seem to still be writing about them a lot.

In case you've been living under a rock or in a coma for the last decade, most critics and media-watchers agree that the current uber-zombie craze in pop culture (books, movies, comics, television, games, trading cards, clothing, food, philosophy, college courses, etc.) is at least partially my fault. Almost fifteen years ago, the publication of my first novel, *The Rising*, coincided with the release of a movie called *28 Days Later* and a comic book called *The Walking Dead*. All three featured different kinds of zombies, which was okay with most people, since nobody else had done much with zombies for the decade or so leading up to their releases. All three were big hits within their respective media. *City of the Dead*, my sequel to *The Rising*, followed soon after, and so did a lot of other books and movies and comics. And they haven't gone away. Indeed, there seem to be more of them than ever. There are now publishing companies that publish nothing but zombie literature and authors who write about nothing but the living dead.

I had a chance to do the same. In truth, I could have probably made a very good living (meaning a lot more money than what I make now) doing for zombies what Anne Rice did for vampires, and just written zombie novels, but doing so didn't appeal to me. I didn't want to be typecast. I didn't want to become 'The Zombie Guy.' I wanted to write about other monsters and other situations. So I did. And a lot of other people came along and wrote about zombies instead and made a lot of money doing so, while I wrote about things like ghouls and un-killable Russian mobsters and giant, carnivorous earthworms. In hindsight, those other authors might have been a lot smarter than me.

Occasionally, I did indeed return to writing about zombies. I tried my hand at the traditional "Romero-style" undead (with *Dead Sea*) and returned to the world of *The Rising* with a collection of thirty-two original short stories that all took place in that world, called *The Rising: Selected Scenes From the End of the World*. After that, I decided I was really burned out on zombies. Upon reflection, though, I wasn't so much burned out as I was written-out. I didn't want to just repeat the same story over and over again (which is the risk any author or filmmaker runs when dealing with the undead—or any other genre trope). So I proclaimed myself as 'DONE WITH ZOMBIES.'

And I fucking damn well meant it, too…

…except that people kept offering me money to write about zombies one more time. It's hard to say no to money. I like money. I'm a big fan. With two ex-wives and two sons and a metric fuck-ton of debt, I have no choice but to be a big fan of money. So I've returned to zombies a few more times since then, but only when I thought I had an original idea (such as my comic series *The Last Zombie*, which deals with the aftermath of a zombie apocalypse, after the dead are all dead again) and my novel *Entombed* (which takes place in the world of *Dead Sea* and deals with bunker mentality and the psychological ramifications of surviving a zombie apocalypse). But when I pause to consider those two works, it occurs to me that the zombies are nothing more than window dressing. They appear only briefly in *Entombed*, and don't appear at all in *The Last Zombie* (except in flashbacks). So maybe I really am done with zombies, after all.

What I'm not done with, however, is characters. The Reverend Thomas Martin has always been a personal favorite character of mine (along with a handful of other characters such as Adam Senft, Levi Stoltzfus, Timmy Graco, Teddy Garnett, Whitey Putin and Tony Genova). I'm quite fond of Reverend Martin, and nobody was more surprised than I was when—SPOILER ALERT—he died in the first few chapters of *City of the Dead*. I did not see that coming.

I've written a lot of novels since then, but occasionally, I'd find my thoughts returning to Martin. I knew his story wasn't over yet, even though he was dead. I knew there was a lot more to him than what readers saw in *The Rising* and *City of the Dead*. I knew that some of the more interesting parts of his saga took place before the events in those books, and I'm glad I've finally gotten the chance to write about them here in this prequel.

The Rising: Deliverance isn't a story about zombies. It's a story about people. And fate. And faith. And doubt. And all the other things that define us and make us human. It's a story of the things that shaped Reverend Thomas Martin before readers met him in *The Rising*. It's about the real reason he agreed to go with Jim in search of Danny. You might have enjoyed it. You might not have. But I can tell you that I enjoyed writing it.

I wrote this prequel in 2010, which was a terrible year for me. At the time, I'd been seriously considering retiring from writing. There were times, when the going got especially tough, that urge to quit was overwhelmingly strong, and you will never know how close I came to acting on it. But instead of running away, I fled to the place where it all began—the world of *The Rising*—and returned to a character that has always been near in my head and my heart—the Reverend Thomas Martin. Writing about him restored my faith in what I do and gave me hope that it's worthwhile. Seeing him again, if only for this brief novella, gave me my own form of deliverance. And I needed that.

I hope it did something for you, as well.

As always, thanks for buying this and for all of your support. It is always appreciated. I'll keep writing them if you keep reading them.

Brian Keene
December 2014

AUTHOR'S NOTE

As a special bonus, here are two short stories featuring another character from the world of *The Rising* – Ob, a member of the Thirteen and the malevolent leader of the Siqqusim.

The first story, "The Resurrection and The Life", is a remake of chapter eleven of the Book of John, which tells the story of how Jesus raised Lazarus from the dead. Of course, unlike the version in the Bible, this retelling features the addition of Ob.

The second story, "The Siqqusim Who Stole Christmas", also stars Ob, but in addition, it guest stars two other recurring characters of mine—Tony Genova and Vince Napoli. These organized crime enforcers have previously appeared in the short stories "Crazy for You" and "Marriage Causes Cancer in Rats", as well as the novels *Clickers II, Clickers III*, and *Clickers vs. Zombies* (the latter of which also features Ob).

Enjoy!

THE RESURRECTION AND THE LIFE

And so the Jewish priests accused the Rabbi, who was called Jesus, of blasphemy and tried to stone him. Jesus and his disciples fled Jerusalem for their very lives. Escaping to the borders of Judea, they crossed over the Jordan River to the place where John had been baptized in the early days. There they set up camp, safe from the law, and Jesus began to teach again.

Many curious people came to the site over the next four days. Some just wanted to listen to what Jesus had to say. Others had heard rumors of miracles—that he'd made a blind man see, touched a lame little girl and commanded her to throw away her crutches, cast out demons and walked across water. They flocked to the riverbank hoping for a glimpse, hoping to see something miraculous so that they could tell their children and grandchildren about it in years to come. They longed to say, "I was there the day Jesus of Nazareth made the sky rain blood. He split a rock with his staff and brought forth water. He touched your father's stump and his arm sprang forth anew. Serpents flee before him."

At first, they were disappointed. That emotion soon waned. Jesus performed no miracles during those four days. He didn't have to. No matter what their reasons for attending, once the throng heard him speak, they believed. His voice was melodious and assured, and the strength of his convictions shone through in every word. Unlike the prophets who held court in the desert or in the bazaars and alleyways, Jesus appeared sane. Likeable. His charisma was infectious.

When John had taught on this same riverbank in earlier

years, he'd prophesied about the Messiah. Many of the older members in the crowd had heard John's predictions regarding Jesus, and after listening to Jesus speak they said, "Though John never performed a miraculous sign, all that he said about this man, Jesus of Nazareth, was true. He really is the Son of God. The Messiah walks among us."

On the fifth day, a messenger from the Judean village of Bethany crossed the border and entered the camp. Word spread through the crowd that he was seeking Jesus. Worried that the messenger might actually be an assassin sent by the priests, Peter, one of Jesus' disciples, met with the man and demanded that the message be given to him instead. But Jesus overheard this and granted the messenger an audience, telling Peter, "If any come seeking me, you must show them the way."

Jesus and the messenger drew away from the others, and Jesus offered the man water and bread, saying, "I can feed your hunger and thirst, if you will only partake."

When he was sated, the man delivered his message.

"Rabbi," he said, "I have tidings from Mary and her sister, Martha, who reside in the village of Bethany. It concerns their brother, Lazarus."

Jesus knew Mary, Martha, and Lazarus very well. All three were dear and faithful friends of his. Many months ago, as Jesus and his disciples were traveling through Judea, they'd come to a village where a woman named Martha opened her home to them. Jesus taught from Martha's home for many days. Her sister, Mary, had sat at his feet and listened to what he said. Martha had been unable to partake in the teachings because she was distracted by all the preparations that had to be made in order to feed all twelve of Jesus' entourage. She'd come to Jesus and asked, "Lord, don't you care that my sister has left me to do the work by myself? Tell her to help me!"

When he heard this, Jesus said, "Martha, you are worried

and upset about many things, but only one thing is needed. Mary has chosen what is better, and it will not be taken away from her."

At first, Martha had not understood his meaning, but when at last the knowledge dawned on her, she laughed. The sound had filled the Son of God's heart with happiness. He loved them both, and loved their brother Lazarus most of all, for he was a good man and had not been offended when Mary poured perfume on Jesus' feet and wiped them with her hair. Lazarus had understood the symbolism and blessed it with his acceptance rather than demanding blood.

Jesus smiled at the memory.

"Lord?" The messenger shuffled his feet in the sand, unsure if Jesus had heard him.

"What news from Mary and Martha?" Jesus asked. "What news of Lazarus?"

"The sisters have commanded me to say, 'Lord, the one you love is sick'."

When he heard this, Jesus patted the messenger's hand. "This sickness will not end in death. No, it is for God's glory so that God's Son may be glorified through it."

***

Jesus loved Martha, Mary and Lazarus. Yet when he heard that Lazarus was sick, he stayed where he was two more days, teaching upon the banks of the Jordan, because he was afraid.

"Surely, he will go to aid his friends," whispered Judas. "He would not let death claim a man such as Lazarus."

"Our Lord cannot return," Peter said. "Have you forgotten? Bethany is in the heart of Judea. We have just fled that place for our very lives. To return now would mean certain death."

Many of the people who had come to hear Jesus out of

curiosity had ended up staying, forsaking their farms and families so that they could gain knowledge and understanding.

On the seventh day, just as the sun rose over the hills, Jesus called his disciples together. They sat around the fire and shared a wineskin and bread. The assembled crowd was still sleeping.

When they had broken their fast, Jesus said to his disciples, "Let us go back to Judea."

"But Rabbi," Paul exclaimed, "a short while ago the Jews tried to stone you, and yet you are going back there?"

Jesus nodded. "We must return. Our friend Lazarus is sick."

"Then we shall travel under the cover of darkness," Matthew suggested.

"No, Matthew," Jesus said. "That is not the way. Are there not twelve hours of daylight? A man who walks by day will not stumble, for he sees by this world's light. It is when he walks by night that he stumbles, for he has no light."

Paul stood up. "I still do not think it is a good idea, Lord."

Judas poured river water on the campfire and stirred the ashes. The rest of the disciples grumbled among themselves.

Jesus insisted. "Our friend Lazarus has fallen asleep; but I am going to Bethany to wake him up."

"Lord," Luke said, "if Lazarus sleeps, then he will get better. We should let him rest."

"That is not the sleep I speak of. Lazarus is dead, and for your sake I am glad that I was not there, so that you may believe. But enough talk for now. Let us go to him."

Jesus stood up and prepared to leave. He moved amongst the crowd, wishing them well and imparting his blessing. Some of the people wept when they heard that he was leaving, for they knew what the Jewish priests would do if he were caught.

Jesus reached the bank of the river and turned around. He called out, "I go to Judea."

"Then you go to your death, my Lord," Judas whispered.

Thomas, who was also called Didymus, said to the rest of the disciples, "Let us also go, that we may die with him."

***

When they arrived, Lazarus had already been dead and in his tomb for four days.

Bethany was less than two miles from Jerusalem, and many Jews had come to Martha and Mary to comfort them in the loss of their brother. They brought whispers and gossip of Jesus' arrival—how he and his followers were approaching in broad daylight, marching down the main road in plain defiance of the priests. When Martha heard that Jesus was coming, she went out to meet him, but Mary stayed at home.

Jesus greeted Martha. "It is good to see you."

The distraught woman did not return his smile, nor would she meet his eyes.

"What troubles you?" Jesus asked.

"Lord, if you had been here, my brother would not have died. But I know that even now God will give you whatever you ask."

"And what would you have me ask of my Father, dear Martha?"

Martha lowered her head again. Her voice was barely a whisper. "That He not have taken Lazarus from me."

"Your brother will rise again," Jesus told her.

"I know he will rise again in the resurrection at the last day."

"But," Jesus said, "I am the resurrection and the life. He who believes in me will live, even though he dies; and whoever lives and believes in me will never die. Do you believe this, Martha?"

"Yes, Lord," she replied, "I believe that you are the Christ, the Son of God, who was to come into the world."

"Then let not your heart be troubled. You will see your brother again. Now where is Mary?"

"She is at our home, Lord. I should make haste there as well, to prepare for you and your disciples."

Sighing, Jesus eyed the crowd that had gathered to see him. "We shall follow along behind you as we are able."

Martha ran home ahead of them. Mary was still in mourning, and had not moved from the straw mat in the corner. She was surrounded by many friends, all of them offering comfort, and yet no comfort did she find. Martha went to her sister's side.

"The Rabbi is here and he is asking for you."

When Mary heard this, she got up quickly and went out to meet him. The people who had been comforting Mary noticed how hastily she left. They followed her, assuming she was going to the tomb to mourn her brother there.

Jesus and his disciples had not yet entered the village, and were still at the place where Martha had met them. Jesus was giving an impromptu lesson to the assembled crowd. When Mary reached the place and saw Jesus, she fell at his feet and wept.

"Lord, if you had been here, my brother would not have died."

Mary's friends grew sullen and whispered among themselves about the influence Jesus had on her. Several of them began to cry as well, overcome with sorrow for their friend, Lazarus. They grieved for the two sisters. Both had believed until the very end that this son of a carpenter—this Nazarene—would somehow save Lazarus. But he had not. And now Lazarus was dead.

Jesus was deeply moved by their tears, and his spirit was troubled. "Where have you laid him?"

"Come and see, Lord," Mary replied. Her face was wet, her eyes red.

They walked along the road and Jesus wept. As they

passed by the sisters' house, Martha joined the procession, assuming that Jesus wished to bid his respects to the deceased. More villagers followed along, and the disciples grew nervous, certain that word of their presence would reach the priests in Jerusalem soon.

One of Mary's friends watched Jesus cry, and said, "See how he loved Lazarus! He did not mean for him to die."

But another of them said, "Could not he who opened the eyes of the blind man have kept this man from dying? That is what the sisters believed."

Jesus did not respond. His tears fell like rain, spattering the dry, dusty ground.

Father, he prayed, *forgive me that I did not want to return to Judea. I knew what awaited me here—the beginning of the end. I was fearful of death. I am sorry. I now follow your will, though I am still afraid...*

***

They came to the tomb, a cave with a massive stone blocking the entrance. Even with the entrance sealed as such, the smell of rot and decay hung thick in the air.

"Take away the stone," Jesus said.

"But, Lord," said Martha, "by this time there is a bad odor, for he has been in there four days."

"Did I not tell you that if you believed, you would see the glory of God?"

"Yes."

"Then take away the stone."

Several of the disciples did as he commanded, grunting with the effort. They rolled the boulder away, revealing a yawning, black crevice. The stench that wafted out was horrible and many in the crowd turned away. The foul miasma did not seem to bother Jesus. He stepped towards the opening and looked up into the sky.

"Father," he said, "I thank you that you have heard me. I knew that you always hear me, but I said this for the benefit of the people standing here, that they may believe that you sent me."

He moved closer still. He trod on old bones and his sandals crushed them into powder. Jesus bowed his head in prayer. The crowd watched, fascinated.

Then Jesus shouted, "Lazarus, come out!"

No one moved. They stared in shocked silence as a sound came from inside the tomb—a soft whisper, cloth on rock. A bent form shuffled towards the entrance and many of the onlookers were afraid. Somewhere near the back of the crowd, a child began to cry. A cloud passed over the sun, and when it had passed, the dead man staggered out of the tomb, his hands and feet wrapped with strips of soiled linen, and a bloody cloth around his face. His bodily fluids had oozed into the rags, crusting them with gore.

Gasping, the crowd shrank away. But Mary, Martha, and the disciples surged forward, shouting with joy.

Jesus said, "Take off the grave clothes and let him go."

They stripped the dirty linens from Lazarus's body and when his sisters saw his face, they wept with happiness.

"Oh, brother," Mary cried. "You are returned to us. We are blessed. Truly, the Lord is mighty."

Lazarus stared at them, blinking, as if trying to remember who they were. Then he smiled.

"Hello, my sisters. It is good to see you."

Jesus was startled. His disciples noticed, but no one else among the crowd did; they were too busy celebrating Lazarus's resurrection. Mary and Martha knelt at their brother's feet and kissed his hands. Lazarus ignored them, his gaze settling on Jesus.

"Thank you," the dead man said, grinning. *"Thank you for this release."*

Jesus did not reply. He tried to appear happy but his

smile faltered. His demeanor troubled the disciples, and they pulled him aside.

"What is it, Lord," asked Mark. "Are you not happy to see our friend?"

"He is not our friend," Jesus whispered.

"But Rabbi," Judas exclaimed, "this is Lazarus that stands before us, resurrected by your will and strength. This is a sign of your testimony."

Jesus shook his head. "This is not what I summoned. This is something else."

"What, Lord?" Matthew glanced back at the crowd, watching Lazarus move among them.

Jesus frowned. "Speak softly, so that none other shall hear. This is not our friend Lazarus. Something else inhabits the temple of his body. Something that it is not given to me to have power over."

Luke was incredulous. "Lord, even the demons submit to us in your name. You have power over everything."

"No," Jesus replied, "I have given you authority to trample on snakes and scorpions and to overcome all the power of the enemy; nothing will harm you. However, do not rejoice that the spirits submit to you, but rejoice that your names are written in heaven. I saw Satan fall like lightning from heaven. I saw his army fall with him. But there were Thirteen that did not fall, yet neither did they serve my Father. My Father has no power over their kind. Great among the Thirteen is Ob, the Obot. He is lord of the Siqqusim and it is given to him the power to reside in the dead."

"Then cast him out, Lord," Judas said. "Force him to flee our friend's body."

"I cannot," Jesus said, "for as I said, I have no power over him."

"But why is he here?"

"My Father is displeased, for I feared to enter Judea again."

Frowning in confusion, the disciples watched Lazarus and the Jews. The dead man moved spryly, his limbs showing none of the stiffness that came with death.

"I am hungry," Ob croaked with Lazarus's mouth. *"Who among you shall feed me?"*

"We shall prepare a great feast for you, brother," Martha cried, "to celebrate your return to us."

"Yes," Mary agreed. "We shall all feed you."

Ob smiled at this news, and stared at Jesus.

"Will you not come dine at my sister's table?" Ob asked, laughing.

"I will not."

"You will miss a rich meal." Lazarus put his arm around Mary's shoulder and leaned close to her. *"Delicious and succulent. Truly a tantalizing feast for the senses."*

Jesus stirred. "Come and walk with me, Lazarus. Let us give thanks for your return."

Ob's smile faltered. Noticing that the crowd was watching him, he held his head high and walked over to where Jesus stood. The disciples drew away from them, leaving the two alone.

"You befoul this body," Jesus spat. "You defile my Father's glory."

Ob leaned close, his stinking breath hot on his adversary's face. "Your Father is disappointed with you. Since the day you turned fourteen, you have known this time would come. When the angel appeared to you and revealed your destiny, you were distraught. Since then, you have accepted God's will. You knew that in this, your thirty-second year, you would be asked to work this miracle. You would be asked to intercede on behalf of your friends. You would return to Judea, be betrayed by the one you call Judas, and die at the hands of the Jews. You knew your Father's will, and yet you balked. You delayed, because you did not wish to return. Did not wish to set these events into motion. And thus, He has sent me so that you will not forget: It is His will that you serve."

"You lie."

"I am not the Master of Lies. That is your older brother, the Morningstar."

Jesus glanced over Ob's shoulder. Martha and Mary were waiting.

"If you harm them," he whispered, "then know this. I will—"

"Do nothing," Ob interrupted. "I am forbidden to harm them. If I do, I shall be returned to the Void. Your Father may be powerless, but He has human agents who know the way."

They glared at each other, unblinking, and it was Jesus who looked away first.

"I understand now," Jesus told his disciples. "My Father's will has been made clear to me. I understand why He commanded us to return to this place. I understand all that will transpire. And know this, Judas. I forgive you."

Judas was taken aback. "Forgive me, Lord? For what? Do you not know that I love you? That I serve you faithfully?"

Jesus' smile was sad. His eyes grew wet again. Instead of responding to Judas, he bid farewell to the sisters and told his disciples to follow him.

"Where are we going, Lord?" Thomas asked.

"I must go into the desert and pray. We cannot be here after dark."

"Lord," Peter insisted, "we must stay and fight him for the glory of God."

"No," Jesus said. "My Father has forbidden it."

***

That night, there was a great celebration in the village, and all hailed Lazarus's return. After the celebrants had fallen asleep, satiated on lamb and duck and wine, Ob moved among them and began to feed. He plucked sleeping babes from their mother's breasts and drank their blood. He then turned to the mothers, nuzzling at their teats as they slept, before sinking his teeth into the soft flesh. Screams ripped through the night. Ob's feeding frenzy continued. He ripped the arms from men and wielded the severed limbs like clubs, striking at others. He chewed the face off a beggar, tore into stomachs, gouged eyeballs and ate them like grapes, bit into Adam's apples as if they were real apples, and left a trail of gore and offal behind him. Bethany became a place of slaughter. He licked the scabs of lepers, skewered children on spears, and even feasted on the livestock and pets.

When he was satisfied, Ob vanished into the night, intent on finding the necessary ingredients to open a portal and free his brethren from their imprisonment in the Void.

The cries of the dying and wounded drifted into the desert, and when Jesus heard them, he wept again.

***

Many of the Jews who had come to visit Mary, and had seen what Jesus did, put their faith in him after the resurrection. But when the first light of dawn lit upon the massacre, they went to the Pharisees and told them what had occurred. None of them thought to connect Lazarus to the crimes. Instead, they assumed it was a demon. They didn't know how right they were.

The chief priests and the Pharisees called a meeting of the Sanhedrin.

"What are we accomplishing?" they asked. "Here is this man, Jesus of Nazareth, performing many miraculous signs. If we let him go on like this, everyone will believe in him, and then the Romans will come and take away both our place and our nation. Surely, he has loosed a demon upon us, as punishment for speaking against him."

Caiaphas, the high priest, spoke up. "The Romans shall do nothing. I have a plan. It is better that one man should die for the people than that the whole nation perish. We shall slay this Rabbi, and we shall slay this demon he has summoned forth. We shall also slay this man, Lazarus, whom has returned from the dead."

When word of this reached Jesus, he called his disciples together. "We can no longer move about publicly among the Jews. Instead, we will withdraw to a region near the desert, in a village called Ephraim."

And so they did. Mary and Martha wondered what had become of their brother. When Jesus and his disciples disappeared, they assumed Lazarus had gone with them. Meanwhile, Ob roamed the sands and mountains of Judea, raiding and feasting in the night and hiding during the day, plotting to unleash the Siqqusim. Word spread that a demon was on the loose, and people slept with a guard posted. Children were warned not to stray far from home.

***

When it was almost time for Passover, many came to Jerusalem for their ceremonial cleansing. The crowds kept looking for Jesus, and as they stood in the temple, they asked one another, "What do you think? Isn't he coming to the Feast at all?" The chief priests and Pharisees had given orders that if anyone found out where Jesus was, they should report it so that he could be arrested.

Eventually, Jesus returned to Bethany. His spirits seemed low, and he did not teach. The sisters gave a dinner in his honor. Much to Mary and Martha's delight, Lazarus arrived as well, and reclined at the table with Jesus. They could not understand why the disciples met his arrival with dread and shrank away from him. Lazarus's flesh, while not marred, was sallow and ripe. Mary put a few drops of pure nard, an expensive perfume, on her brother's head. Then she poured some on Jesus' feet and wiped them with her hair. The house was filled with the fragrance.

Judas objected. "Why was this perfume not sold, and the money given to the poor? It was worth a year's wages."

"Leave her alone," Jesus said. "It was intended that she should save this perfume for the day of my burial. You will always have the poor, Judas, but you will not always have me."

Ob laughed, loud and boisterous. The dinner guests were shocked, but Jesus ignored him.

"The hour has come," Jesus continued, "for the Son of Man to be glorified. Unless a kernel of wheat falls to the ground and dies, it remains only a single seed. But if it dies, it produces many seeds."

"And one day," Ob interrupted, *"all will die, and the seeds of my kind's revenge shall be sown."*

Jesus' demeanor changed. He whirled on Lazarus.

"Silence your tongue!"

Ob leaned close and whispered, *"Caution, Nazarene. I am forbidden to harm the sisters, but your Father said nothing of your precious disciples. I can eat their bodies in remembrance of you."*

Ignoring him, Jesus turned back to his listeners. "The man who loves life will lose it, while the man who hates life in this world will keep it for eternal life. Whoever serves me must follow me; and where I am, my servant also will be. My Father will honor those who serve me.

There came a loud, insistent knock at the door. All of the assembled jumped, startled. The knock came again. Mary opened the door. A priest and four soldiers pushed into the home.

"Where is Jesus of Nazareth?"

"I am he."

"And where is Lazarus of Bethany?"

Ob rose. *"I am he."*

The priest appraised them both. "And you, Jesus, claim you brought this man, Lazarus, back from the dead."

"I did, by the Glory of God."

"Then you blaspheme."

"If you have eyes," Jesus said, "let them see. Follow me."

He strode past the armed men, and they did not molest him. The priest followed him outside, along with the disciples, the sisters, and the other guests. Ob remained inside. Jesus turned back to the house.

"Lazarus, come forth."

Ob's host body's legs moved without him willing them. He glanced down in panicked confusion.

"What is this?"

His arms and hands defied him and opened the door. He strode out into the streets and cursed Jesus' name.

"What trickery is this?"

"No trickery," Jesus said. "I cannot command thee, but it suddenly occurs to me that I can command the flesh you inhabit."

Many among the crowd were confused, but did not intercede.

Jesus turned to the priest. "I brought this man back from the dead. Is he not now marked for death because of it?"

The priest nodded.

"And if I did it again, would you not then believe?"

"What are you saying, Rabbi?"

"Carry out your sentence. Slay him. Then I shall bring him back and you shall see."

"Wait," Ob shouted. *"You cannot—"*

The priest nodded at the soldiers. "Make it so."

Mary and Martha averted their eyes, but were not afraid, because they had faith in the Lord. A soldier stepped forward, armor clanking, and thrust a spear into Lazarus's chest. Ob grasped the shaft and grunted. The crowd gasped.

"He lives," they murmured. "He does not fall."

"His head," the priest commanded. "He cannot survive that."

Ob's eyes grew wide. *"No. Strike not my head. Do not—"*

A second soldier drew his short sword and plunged it through the back of Lazarus's head. He pushed hard, pierced the skull, and slid it the rest of the way in. The sound of splintering bone filled the air. Lazarus dropped, and Ob was dispatched. He screamed with rage, but none save Jesus could hear him.

As he fled, Ob's spirit whispered in Jesus' ear. *"You know what fate your Father plans for thee. I shall be there, waiting. And after your spirit has fled, when your discarded flesh hangs from the cross, I will take it for my own. When you rise from the dead, it shall be me inside this bag of skin and blood and bones. You may be the Life, but I am the Resurrection."*

The priest looked at the corpse lying in the street and said to Jesus, "Now, if you are whom you say, bring him back."

Jesus folded his arms. "I will not. For you have eyes but do not see. I am the resurrection and the life, but your lack of faith blinds you."

"This Rabbi is touched in the head," the priest said. "Nothing more. He is not the Messiah. He is a simple madman."

After the priest and soldiers had departed, and Mary and Martha wept for the second time over their brother's fallen form, Jesus turned to the disciples.

"Now my heart is troubled, and what shall I say? 'Father, save me from this hour?' No, it was for this very reason I came to this hour. Father, glorify your name!"

Then a voice came from heaven, "I HAVE GLORIFIED IT, AND WILL AGAIN."

Some in the crowd thought the voice was thunder. Others

said it was an angel.

Jesus said, "This voice was for your benefit, not mine. Now is the time for judgment on this world; now the prince of this world will be driven out. But when I am lifted up from the earth, I will draw all men to myself. You are going to have the light just a little while longer. Walk while you have the light, before darkness overtakes you all. For one day, it will. Darkness will descend upon this entire world, and shall not be lifted. That shall be the time of the Rising. Put your trust in the light while you have it, so that you may become sons of light, and not be left behind as the dead."

When he had finished speaking, Jesus left Bethany and hid himself from them. In the desert, powerless to act against Ob, he turned to the ways of man. He performed a secret spell, passed down from Solomon, taken from the *Daemonolateria,* and cast Ob's disembodied spirit into the Void.

Judas, who was hiding behind a stone, saw Jesus work the forbidden rites and was appalled. He had believed his Rabbi to be the Son of God, and had believed that Jesus' powers came from the Holy Spirit. But now, here he was working arcane magicks.

At that moment, Judas' heart was filled with resentment, and he vowed to turn Jesus over to the priests.

And in the Void, Ob wailed and raged and waited for the death of light and the time of the Rising.

THE SIQQUISM WHO STOLE CHRISTMAS

Ob entered the fat man's body at thirty-thousand feet. After taking control of the corpse, he glanced over the side of the craft. A snow-covered landscape zipped by far below. The wind howled in his ears as he passed through a cloud. The dampness chilled him.

It was nighttime. Stars cast their cold, lonely lights from far above. Ob hated each and every one of them.

The Lord of the Siqqusim stared at his reflection in the vehicle's polished silver handrails. Outwardly, the man's body wasn't much. A long, white beard, bordering on unkempt, dangled from a face whose centerpiece was a bulbous red nose. The fat man was adorned in a red suit, matching the color of his nose, like the garb of a jester or clown. He smelled faintly of gingerbread. Ob scanned the body's memories, picking through the brain like it was a filing cabinet, searching for clues to this new host's identity.

The fat man had died of an aneurism. He'd been—

Ob's laughter was louder than the roaring wind. Had the rest of the Thirteen been present, they'd have shared in his amusement.

This host body had suffered an impossible aneurism—impossible since the fat man was supposed to be immortal. He was one of the old gods, known to various tribes as Santa Claus, Kris Cringle, the Dark Elf, Father Christmas and other, long-forgotten names. He was not able to die, and yet he had—the victim of a slow, eons-long spiritual rot. Ob had seen it before, in Rome and Greece and elsewhere.

Santa Claus had died from the cancer of non-belief.

All gods existed on belief. It was their power. Their

food. The more people that believed in them, the stronger they became. But when they lost favor with their devout followers, when people stopped believing in them and began worshipping other deities, the gods grew weaker. If it continued long enough, the gods could die. It had happened to Zeus. To Odin. To countless others, both remembered and forgotten. History was written in the blood of forgotten pantheons. They'd been replaced with new gods. Shinier gods. Gods of medicine and science and peace.

Of course, humanity hadn't realized that Claus was a god. They just thought of him as some kindly old legend, a story to tell children. A benevolent figurehead. A marketing icon. Which was fine, since millennia ago, he'd been that very thing—a god of production and commerce. Claus had transformed over time, altering his identity and duties to suit the ever-changing demands of his fickle believers. All gods did so, when required. They had no choice. Beholden to the whims of the faithful, even the gods had to adapt or die.

Ob and the rest of the Thirteen were not gods, and thus, they had no such weaknesses. The Thirteen scoffed at the inferior beings—gods, angels, demons, devils. All of them were amateurs. They were mere children, battling for scraps from the Creator's table, fighting for the right to be chained to the desires of humanity, sentenced to obey their believer's prayers, for to do so was to reward their faith. Rewarding humanity's faith kept the belief strong—and thus, kept the gods strong.

Ob longed for the day when he could destroy them all. He would kick the Creator from the throne and ascend for himself.

But not yet.

One planet, one reality, at a time. Ob and his fellow Siqqusim had just finished with another Earth, slaughtering the last of the humans and making a mockery with their corpses. While his brothers, Ab and Api, took over, Ob had led the Siqqusim into the Great Labyrinth between worlds, moving on to this level of existence.

Finished with Claus's memories, Ob looked around the sled. It was piled high with colorfully-wrapped boxes and bags. The vast storage space behind the seat was much bigger inside than it appeared from the outside. Ob knew that if he dived into that mound of presents, he could burrow all night and still not reach the bottom. Leather reigns lay in his lap. Ob picked them up and sleigh-bells jingled. The reigns were tied to nine mangy familiars. Each had taken the earthly form of a reindeer. The familiar at the head of the procession was smaller than the others, but its nose glowed scarlet with arcane energies.

Ob experimented with the reigns. The familiars obeyed his commands, unaware that their master no longer inhabited this obese shell. Ob directed them to land. They dropped out of the sky and soared above a village in the Lapland province of Finland. The sled drifted to a halt in the deep snow. Other than the sleigh's jingling bells, the town was silent. The streets were deserted and the villagers were most likely asleep. Smoke curled from a few chimneys. Many doors and windows were adorned with Christmas decorations. Icicles hung from roofs and gutters.

Ob climbed out of the sled and approached the reindeer. They stomped their hooves and pawed the snow, sensing that something was wrong, but unaware of what it was. Their master smelled different. His aura had vanished.

"Well," Ob said, *"ho, ho, ho and all that. Names have power, so let's get down to the act of naming."* He pointed at each as he spoke. *"Rudolph, Dasher, Dancer, Prancer, Vixen, Comet, Cupid, Donner and Blitzen. Now... do you know who I am?"*

The familiars glanced at each other, snorting in fear.

"I'm the reason for the season." Ob licked his lips. *"Meet the new boss, same as the old boss."*

His teeth flashed in the darkness.

***

Alvar Pokka slept next to his hearth. The embers glowed softly. The warmth eased his aching joints, stiff with arthritis. He was eighty-two years old and had lived in Lapland all of his life. Until that night, Alvar had thought he knew everything there was to know about the region's flora and fauna. But the sound that woke him was like nothing he'd ever heard.

Alvar hadn't known that reindeer could scream.

He crept to the window. The fire's warmth seemed to vanish. Alvar peered out the frosted glass and gasped. Santa Claus was slaughtering his reindeer. One by one, he tore out their throats with his hands and teeth. His white beard had turned crimson, dripping gore. The dead animals dropped to the frozen ground. Steam rose from their corpses.

Then they got up again and prowled through the snow-filled streets.

Soon, Alvar's shrieks mingled with the rest of the villagers' screams.

***

Tony Genova bolted upright in his bed, wondering if he'd screamed out loud. His heart hammered in his chest, and his ears rang. He glanced around the dimly lit room. His long-time associate, the severely overweight Vince Napoli, sat in a chair, eating junk food and watching television. Vince turned when Tony cleared his throat.

"Sorry," Vince said. "Did the TV wake you up?"

Tony shook his head, waiting for his racing pulse to slow down. He slid out from under the covers, fully dressed, and put his feet on the floor. A log on the fireplace popped, sending a shower of sparks drifting up into the chimney. He smoothed his tie and noticed that his hand was trembling.

94

"Jeez, Tony! You're sweating like a pig. You okay?"

Tony nodded. "I'm fine. Just had a bad dream is all."

"It's that shit they fed us for dinner," Vince mused, his eyes not leaving the television. "You should have brought some stuff from the States, like I did. Sleep like a baby."

"No thanks. We're in fucking Finland—I want to eat like they do. You go to Italy, you eat Doritos?"

Vince nodded.

"Okay," Tony rolled his eyes. "Maybe you do. But other people don't. People go to Italy, they want to eat Italian food. Same thing here."

Vince didn't reply. Secretly, Tony thought he might be right. The village only had one place to eat—a rustic tavern with a few elderly patrons. Tony and Vince didn't speak the language, and their translator, a young man named Tjers, had met with an unfortunate accident after offering Tony a blow job, so they'd had to muddle through the menu. Tony ended up getting a boiled sheep's head on a plate. It stared at him with big mournful eyes while he ate it. What kind of country was this where they left the eyes in your fucking dinner?

And who the hell ate sheep *heads*, anyway?

Tony sighed. What was supposed to be a simple job had turned into a cluster-fuck. It had seemed so straightforward. Travel from the United States to the Savukoski county of Lapland, Finland, which was right on the border with Russia. Meet up with Tjers. Wait for Otar, who was based in Murmansk Oblast, to cross the border, and then make the exchange—money and heroin for a dozen vials of black-market Soviet-era anthrax—a weaponized strain that their employer, Mr. Marano of the Marano crime family, was anxious to obtain. Once the exchange had been made, Otar would fuck off back to Russia, and Tony and Vince were supposed to cross the Korvatunturi mountains, meet up with their transport, and deliver the anthrax back to the States.

Now they were holed up in a converted bedroom in the

tavern's attic. Tjers was dead and buried in the snow, and Otar hadn't shown. They had no one to guide them over the mountain path, and it looked like they were going home empty-handed—if they made it home at all. Their employer was going to be pissed. He didn't like mishaps or mistakes. Their asses were grass and Marano was the lawnmower, unless Tony figured out how to salvage this whole mess.

Merry fucking Christmas.

On the television, cartoon characters jabbered in Finnish.

"All things considered," Tony muttered, "I'd rather be in fucking Pittsburgh."

"What was the dream about?" Vince asked.

Tony watched his obese partner shovel three double-stuffed Oreo cookies into his mouth at once, and sighed again.

"We were sitting in this little cafe in Atlantic City, waiting for Frankie Spicolli to show up. Then a bunch of crab-things straight out of a bad Sci-Fi Channel movie showed up and started killing people. They looked like a cross between a crab, lobster and scorpion."

"Then what happened?"

Tony got out of bed and stretched. Then he smoothed his suit.

"Something about a fucking hurricane or some shit. I don't remember. What the hell are you watching?"

Vince shrugged. "I don't know. It ain't in English. Pretty good, though. Kind of reminds me of Thomas the Tank Engine, except it's got chicks in it. Look at the tits on her!"

"Very nice."

"I was hoping they'd show that Rudolph cartoon."

"The one with the Bumble?"

Vince's eyes lit up. "Yeah, that's the one! I always liked Bumble when I was a kid."

Probably cause you're about the same size, Tony thought. Then he said, "I liked Herbie, the elf that wanted to be a dentist. But then they did that stupid fucking sequel, with the Baby fucking New Year. Ruined the whole thing."

Vince turned back to the television. "Seems like there'd be some kind of special program on, what with it being Christmas Eve and all. Santa lives near here, you know?"

"What?"

"Santa Claus," Vince explained. "Everybody knows his reindeer stay in Finland during the year. There aren't any reindeer at the North Pole."

Tony paused before speaking. "Vince, there ain't no fucking reindeer at the North Pole because there ain't no Santa Claus."

"You sound like my folks, back when I was a teenager. They tried to say there weren't no Santa, too."

"You still believe in Santa Claus?"

"Well, sure, Tony. Don't you?"

"No, I don't. And neither does anybody else over the age of nine. And probably not many of them anymore, either. Hard for a kid to believe in Santa when there's people flying airplanes into buildings and shooting up schools. Jesus fucking Christ, Vince. You believe in the Easter Bunny, too?"

"No." Vince sulked. "Everybody knows the Easter Bunny is make believe. But Santa Claus ain't. He's—"

A scream cut him off, followed by more. A gunshot echoed through the darkness.

"The fuck?" Tony grabbed his Sig-Sauer off the pine nightstand.

More screams and gunshots drifted up from the streets below. The gunfire didn't surprise them. Gun ownership was fairly common in this part of the world, at least by European standards. What startled them was the sudden clattering sound on the roof.

"Turn that shit off," Tony whispered. "Let's see what's the matter."

The television screen went black. Vince pulled his

Kimber 1911 and heaved his prodigious bulk out of the chair, staring at the ceiling. Meanwhile, Tony crept to the window and peered through the blinds.

"Anything?" Vince asked.

Tony shook his head. "Nothing. Sounds like a—wait a fucking second. What the hell?"

Outside, a reindeer was goring an old man in the stomach. When the animal raised its head, entrails hung from its bloody antlers. Before Tony could react, the noise on the roof grew louder.

"Cops?" Vince said, moving towards the chimney.

"Why the fuck would they be coming through the roof, Vince? No. This is something else."

Something jingled in the night. Tony swore it was... sleigh bells.

There was a rustling noise from the roof. Soot and dirt tumbled down the chimney, sprinkling the fire and filling the air with dust. Vince sneezed and Tony's eyes watered. The fire flared, and then sputtered. More debris fell down the chimney. Then they heard a scraping sound and a huge mound of snow fell onto the fire, extinguishing it. Smoke curled from the fireplace. Vince sneezed again and glanced at Tony.

Tony put his finger to his lips, and then motioned towards the fireplace. The two men tiptoed towards it, standing on either side with their handguns at the ready. A long shadow stretched down from the roof. The sleigh bells rang again. Vince started to speak, but Tony shushed him. More snow fell down the shaft, and then something scuffed against the sides of the chimney. The shadow lengthened. Whoever—whatever—was on the roof was coming down.

Moving as one, Vince and Tony backed away from the fireplace. Standing side by side, they extended their arms and clutched their weapons with both hands, holding the barrels steady. Their fingers rested lightly on the triggers. Neither man flinched. They barely breathed. They stood statue-still, waiting.

A figure crashed into the sodden remains of the fire, knocking burnt logs and ashes aside. Crouching, the intruder surveyed the two and cackled.

Tony had seen some bizarre shit in his time. Back home, he'd seen weird lights at night in the woods of LeHorn's Hollow, which was supposed to be haunted. They'd hovered above the ground, no bigger than softballs, before zooming up into the sky and disappearing. There was other oddness, too. He and Vince used the services of a cannibal who lived in York, Pennsylvania to dispose of bodies when the occasion called for it. They'd once had to steal a diamond that burned your skin like acid if you touched it. Then there were the dreams—dreams he'd never told anyone about, not even Vince. Dreams that he'd lived in other times and places. Other worlds. Fighting weird crab-monsters and all sorts of other creatures.

But the figure that emerged from the fireplace was the strangest fucking thing Tony had ever seen.

It looked like Santa Claus—fat (though not as fat as Vince), red suit and hat, rosy cheeks and a beard. But that was where the similarities ended. This garish figure was better suited for Halloween than Christmas. His skin was pale—almost blue. Blood and gore had matted in the beard, and the rosy glow on his cheeks was more dried blood. Most telling was the gunshot wound in his chest. Tony glanced at it, remembering the shot they'd heard earlier. He'd seen men shot there before—had shot men there before. That wasn't a wound you walked around with, let alone crawl across rooftops and drop down chimneys.

Tony tried to speak and couldn't.

Vince summed it up for him, his voice tinged with unexpected delight.

"Santa Claus!"

"Ho, ho fucking ho. Time to die, humans. My brothers need your bodies."

Vince paled. "Santa doesn't curse."

"I am not Santa. I am Ob the Obot, Lord of the Siqqusim and greatest of the Thirteen! Your time is over. For each of you that we kill, one of my kind will take your place. There are so many of us. More than infinity."

Tony smirked. "Are all of them as fat as you?"

The man in red charged towards them.

Tony squeezed the trigger, aiming for the intruder's belly. His mark was true, but Santa barely slowed. He grunted as the bullet slammed into him and ripped through his back, before hitting the brick wall behind him. Santa grinned and took another step forward.

"Tony, you can't shoot Santa Claus!"

Tony barely heard his partner. The sound of the gunshot filled the room. Instead of responding, he fired again. Whoever this guy was, he was still standing despite two shots to the body. This time, he aimed for the face. Santa's grin vanished in a wet explosion of red.

"Shoot the fucker, Vince!"

Santa tried to speak, but his lower jaw was missing. His tongue flopped uselessly, sliding across the shattered remnants of his upper teeth. He seized a fireplace poker and swung it at Tony. Tony dodged the blow, raised his pistol, and fired again. This time, he aimed for the fat man's forehead.

He didn't miss.

Santa uttered a short, garbled moan. Then he fell forward, face first onto the floor. His body twitched once and then he was still. Tony put a foot on his back and fired two more rounds into the back of his head at close range. Then he kicked him. Santa didn't move.

Silence returned. The air was thick with wood smoke and gunpowder. Outside, the screaming continued.

"Jesus..." Vince leaned against the wall with one hand,

panting. "I told you, Tony! See? There is *so* such a thing as Santa Claus."

"No, Vince. There ain't no fucking Santa Claus."

He prodded the corpse with his shoe.

"At least, not anymore."

Tony popped the magazine from his Sig-Sauer, slid a few more bullets into place, and then slammed it back home. He ran to the window and glanced outside. The slaughter continued in the streets as Santa's dead helpers ran riot. Tony grabbed Vince by the arm.

"Come on. Let's go kill ourselves some zombie reindeer."

BRIAN KEENE writes novels, comic books, short fiction, and occasional journalism for money. He is the author of over forty books, mostly in the horror, crime, and dark fantasy genres. His 2003 novel, *The Rising*, is often credited (along with Robert Kirkman's *The Walking Dead* comic and Danny Boyle's *28 Days Later* film) with inspiring pop culture's current interest in zombies. In addition to his own original work, Keene has written for media properties such as *Doctor Who, The X-Files, Hellboy, Masters of the Universe*, and *Superman*.

Several of Keene's novels have been developed for film, including *Ghoul, The Ties That Bind*, and *Fast Zombies Suck*. Several more are in-development or under option. Keene also oversees Maelstrom, his own small press publishing imprint specializing in collectible limited editions, via Thunderstorm Books.

Keene's work has been praised in such diverse places as *The New York Times, The History Channel, The Howard Stern Show, CNN.com, Publisher's Weekly, Media Bistro, Fangoria Magazine*, and *Rue Morgue Magazine*. He has won numerous awards and honors, including the World Horror Grand Master award, two Bram Stoker awards, and a recognition from Whiteman A.F.B. (home of the B-2 Stealth Bomber) for his outreach to U.S. troops serving both overseas and abroad. A prolific public speaker, Keene has delivered talks at conventions, college campuses, theaters, and inside Central Intelligence Agency headquarters in Langley, VA.

The father of two sons, Keene lives in rural Pennsylvania.

deadite press

"Header" Edward Lee - In the dark backwoods, where law enforcement doesn't dare tread, there exists a special type of revenge. Something so awful that it is only whispered about. Something so terrible that few believe it is real. Stewart Cummings is a government agent whose life is going to Hell. His wife is ill and to pay for her medication he turns to bootlegging. But things will get much worse when bodies begin showing up in his sleepy small town. Victims of an act known only as "a Header."

"Red Sky" Nate Southard - When a bank job goes horrifically wrong, career criminal Danny Black leads his crew from El Paso into the deserts of New Mexico in a desperate bid for escape. Danny soon finds himself with no choice but to hole up in an abandoned factory, the former home of Red Sky Manufacturing. Danny and his crew aren't the only living things in Red Sky, though. Something waits in the abandoned factory's shadows, something horrible and violent. Something hungry. And when the sun drops, it will feast.

"Zombies and Shit" Carlton Mellick III - Twenty people wake to find themselves in a boarded-up building in the middle of the zombie wasteland. They soon discover they have been chosen as contestants on a popular reality show called Zombie Survival. Each contestant is given a backpack of supplies and a unique weapon. Their goal: be the first to make it through the zombie-plagued city to the pick-up zone alive. But because there's only one seat available on the helicopter, the contestants not only have to fight against the hordes of the living dead, they must also fight each other.

"Muerte Con Carne" Shane McKenzie - Human flesh tacos, hardcore wrestling, and angry cannibal Mexicans, Welcome to the Border! Felix and Marta came to Mexico to film a documentary on illegal immigration. When Marta suddenly goes missing, Felix must find his lost love in the small border town. A dangerous place housing corrupt cops, borderline maniacs, and something much more worse than drug gangs, something to do with a strange Mexican food cart…

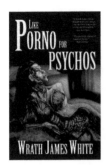
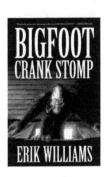

deadite press

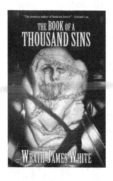

"The Book of a Thousand Sins" Wrath James White - Welcome to a world of Zombie nymphomaniacs, psychopathic deities, voodoo surgery, and murderous priests. Where mutilation sex clubs are in vogue and torture machines are sex toys. No one makes it out alive – not even God himself.
"If Wrath James White doesn't make you cringe, you must be riding in the wrong end of a hearse."
-Jack Ketchum

"Population Zero" Wrath James White - An intense sadistic tale of how one man will save the world through sterilization. *Population Zero* is the story of an environmental activist named Todd Hammerstein who is on a mission to save the planet. In just 50 years the population of the planet is expected to double. But not if Todd can help it. From Wrath James White, the celebrated master of sex and splatter, comes a tale of environmentalism, drugs, and genital mutilation.

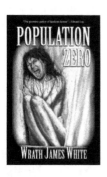

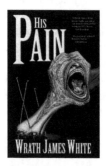

"His Pain" Wrath James White - Life is pain . . . . . . or at least it is for Jason. Born with a rare central nervous disorder, every sensation is pain. Every sound, scent, texture, flavor, even every breath, brings nothing but mind-numbing pain. Until the arrival of Yogi Arjunda of the Temple of Physical Enlightenment. He claims to be able to help Jason, to be able to give him a life of more than agony. But the treatment leaves Jason changed and he wants to share what he learned. He wants to share his pain . . . A novella of pain, pleasure, and transcendental splatter.

"The Vegan Revolution . . . with Zombies" David Agranoff - Thanks to a new miracle drug the cute little pig no longer feels a thing as she is led to the slaughter. The only problem? Once the drug enters the food supply anyone who eats it is infected. From fast food burgers to free-range organic eggs, eating animal products turns people into shambling brain-dead zombies – not even vegetarians are safe!
"A perfect blend of horror, humor and animal activism."
- Gina Ranalli

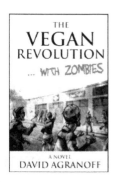

"Whargoul" Dave Brockie - It is a beast born in bullets and shrapnel, feeding off of pain, misery, and hard drugs. Cursed to wander the Earth without the hope of death, it is reborn again and again to spread the gospel of hate, abuse, and genocide. But what if it's not the only monster out there? What if there's something worse? From Dave Brockie, the twisted genius behind GWAR, comes a novel about the darkest days of the twentieth century.

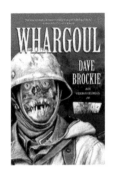

"Super Fetus" Adam Pepper - Try to abort this fetus and he'll kick your ass!

"The story of a self-aware fetus whose morally bankrupt mother is desperately trying to abort him. This darkly humorous novella will surely appall and upset a sizable percentage of people who read it . . . In-your-face, allegorical social commentary."

- BarnesandNoble.com

"Slaughterhouse High" Robert Devereaux - It's prom night in the Demented States of America. A place where schools are built with secret passageways, rebellious teens get zippers installed in their mouths and genitals, and once a year one couple is slaughtered and the bits of their bodies are kept as souvenirs. But something's gone terribly wrong when the secret killer starts claiming a far higher body count than usual . . .

"A major talent!" - Poppy Z. Brite

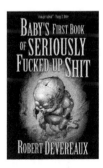

"Baby's First Book of Seriously Fucked-Up Shit" Robert Devereaux - From an orgy between God, Satan, Adam and Eve to beauty pageants for fetuses. From a giant human-absorbing tongue to a place where God is in the eyes of the psychopathic. This is a party at the furthest limits of human decency and cruelty. Robert Devereaux is your host but watch out, he's spiked the punch with drugs, sex, and dismemberment. Deadite Press is proud to present nine stories of the strange, the gross, and the just plain fucked up.

THE VERY BEST IN CULT HORROR

Lightning Source UK Ltd.
Milton Keynes UK
UKHW020758130722
405793UK00008B/529